no drinking no dancing no doctors

BY THE SAME AUTHOR

Fiction
Midnight Feast
The Glass Mountain

Poetry
The Iniscarra Bar and Cycle Rest
All Alcoholics Are Charmers

no drinking no dancing no doctors

martina evans

BLOOMSBURY

First published 2000
This paperback edition published 2001

Copyright © 2000 by Martina Evans

The moral right of the author has been asserted

Bloomsbury Publishing Plc,
38 Soho Square, London W1D 3HB

A CIP record for this book is available
from the British Library

ISBN 0 7475 5227 4

10 9 8 7 6 5 4 3 2 1

Typeset by Hewer Text Ltd, Edinburgh
Printed in England by Clays Ltd, St Ives plc

For Líadaín

ACKNOWLEDGEMENTS

I would like to thank my mother Irene Cotter who brought the nineteen-forties alive for me. I would also like to thank my brother Peter Cotter, Geoffrey Keating at the Irish Embassy, Dr Thomas Bewley, Dr Beulah Bewley, the Arts Council of England for their 1999 Writer's Award and last but not least, Bill Swainson, my editor at Bloomsbury.

Lord G. died of an inflammation of the bowels: so they took them out, and sent them (on account of their discrepancies), separately from the carcass, to England. Conceive a man going one way, and his intestines another, and his immortal soul a third! – was there ever such a distribution? One certainly has a soul; but how it came to allow itself to be enclosed in a body is more than I can imagine.

Byron, letter to Thomas Moore, Venice, 11 April 1817

PART ONE

Chapter One

Danny Fox said that Beulah Kingston was a kleptomaniac about washing. Down at the Cross, they knew that kleptomaniac wasn't the right word for it, but they knew also that it certainly wasn't normal the way Beulah spent hours upon hours every day washing.

Beulah didn't even have a washing machine, just an old-fashioned mangle which was an ornament in itself, according to Danny Fox. After rinsing her wash in the stream that ran under the disused water-mill, Beulah would wring out every article scrupulously with her bare white hands.

These days, people just threw a load into the washing machine whenever they felt like it, they didn't even look out at the weather. There weren't many people about now who walked out on warm windy days and remarked that there was great *drying*.

Not that Beulah talked about drying. But one could see that she was thinking about it. She went in and out of the farmhouse with her nose in the air, her tall thin body held up against the wind, measuring it. Grasping handfuls of linen in her hands and sniffing Persil and Comfort. Fairy Snow and New Lenor. Surf and Woolite. She changed her brands a lot, but she didn't talk about them and she didn't talk about the state of the atmosphere.

3

Beulah did her washing out in the sunshine whenever she got the chance. Sometimes towels which were hard to squeeze and needed violent handling. Delicate washes too. Her sister's lacy nightdresses in lukewarm water and Lux. Danny Fox, her closest neighbour, who never took his cap off from one end of the year to the other (they said that he even slept in it), dared to make remarks when he was poking his fairly long nose over the wall at her.

'Cripes, you're strong!'

'Bejasus, you've a pair of hands on you like a grave digger.'

But Beulah was not to be drawn by Danny Fox, she never answered him when he got smart. Just went on squeezing and wringing, driving him away with her silence.

'It is a fright to God she couldn't even throw me a word and I her neighbour for the best part of sixty year,' Danny Fox said to Nellie Sheehan down at the Cross.

The Cross was Two Mile Cross, a tiny village about seven miles from the town. Nellie Sheehan's grocery was the focal point. It was two miles away from Kingston's and Danny Fox's farm. Danny always bicycled down to the Cross, often just to complain about Beulah, 'She is the hardest, most unnatural woman I've ever met.'

But Nellie Sheehan said, privately, that Danny had always been after Beulah. 'That's what's wrong with him, he's on a constant bed of coals living next door to her and he can't get married now, at least not to a wife with a nose! Do you know that he got the bathroom in 1980 and that bath has been used for storing cans of paint since the day it was put in.'

Beulah said nothing and explained nothing. She, especially, never explained how her young husband, Louis Kingston, had died at the age of twenty, in the full of his health. Or where she went when she disappeared off the farm for three whole days. Danny Fox said that there was another man in it somewhere,

4

but no one was sure about this. They only had Danny's word for it and even he admitted, in the end, that he hadn't seen any strange man hanging around the farm.

'A jealous hallucination,' said Nellie Sheehan.

The bad feeling between Danny Fox and Nellie Sheehan affected the way people thought about Beulah. Because Nellie owned the shop, she had the means of spreading her opinions widely. And the contrast between clean Beulah and dirty Danny swung the balance in Beulah's favour.

'Never so much as a bad word out of her only down on her two knees keeping her house,' the people said.

'Or a good word, either,' said rebellious Danny.

'Spotless to the world!'

'You could eat your dinner off her kitchen floor.'

'But what would you want to do that for?' Danny, as usual, doing himself no favours, moving far too close to people when he was airing his opinions.

Nellie had to open the doors and windows to rid herself of Danny's smell, which got worse and worse as the years went by. And as Nellie herself pointed out, with washing machines and all the mod cons, people's tolerance of dirt had gone away down. 'The people are not prepared to take it and can you blame them if they don't want to come in here and put up with the likes of Danny when they can go into Quinnsworth and do their shopping in peace with beautiful smells and music? Even if those supermarkets are awful places with neither neighbours nor atmosphere.'

'We'll end up closing down over him,' Nellie's daughter Sheila said, running round with the can of Fresh-air.

'And who is the one drawing him on top of us? Asking him questions about the Kingstons, wouldn't you think you'd know better?'

'Well, you tell me, so,' said Sheila.

'There's nothing to tell. The poor creature came back from

5

where ever she was, to live with Hester who'd been called over from the home place. Hester stayed on then to help with the twins, they were born the following year. The shock of her husband's death, that was what made Beulah go off. You have to remember, she was very young when she married Louis Kingston, I would say she was not much more than sixteen.'

'Weren't the Poleites queer, too, when you think of it?'

'They were queer,' said Nellie. 'Very queer,' her face closed up.

'I know that you know stuff and you won't tell me and I'm your own daughter!'

Nellie was taking the meat slicer apart, she was a great one for not hearing what she didn't want to answer. 'Look at the state of the slicer, you wouldn't see that in Quinnsworth's, would you? Get me a bowl of hot soapy water quick, quick!' Nellie gave Sheila a shove, 'Don't you know my livelihood is at stake!'

Nellie was thinking about the mystery of Beulah's nights away from home. Dr Costello had been called out to issue a death certificate for Louis Kingston in the middle of the night. What could have been the rush? Queer business all right. Everything the Poleites did was queer. Joe Costello knocked up Nellie for brandy afterwards, white-faced, thin-lipped. 'Very shaken,' Nellie Sheehan told her husband, who was still alive then, 'He could hardly talk with shock and who could blame him!'

A doctor couldn't sign a death certificate unless the dead person was under his care and, as everyone knew, Louis Kingston could hardly be under doctor's care when he was a Poleite. Of course, if Joe Costello hadn't signed the death certificate, the body would have been taken into the courthouse for an autopsy. Nobody would want to put those queer shy creatures through that ordeal. Besides it would cause a terrible disturbance in the parish. Joe Costello signed the certificate and it was never questioned since.

6

Joe Costello might have talked to Nellie about what had happened, Sheila tormented herself thinking as she swished up a sudsy bowl of hot water and Lemon Quix. But the sad fact was that Nellie was not going to talk to Sheila. 'Tell you things, is it?' Nellie had once said to Sheila. 'And you with a mouth like a torn paper bag!'

How often parents were wrong about their children, thought Sheila. Did her mother think that she had got to the responsible position of nursing sister by going around leaking information? She had studied subjects that her mother wouldn't be able to spell. She knew about things like psychology and postnatal depression. *She* was the one who would be able to analyse the story objectively if she only had a few solid details to go on.

Nellie paused over the meat slicer with her nose wrinkled up, she spoke suddenly about Beulah. It gave Sheila a start.

'Didn't she lose her husband and wasn't the general explanation that she'd gone mad with grief and rushed off into the woods? A woman like that, who never cried or showed emotion. It had to come out some way.'

Joe Costello had told Nellie nothing, but his silence had made a deep impression on her. She had always protected the Poleites as her mother had before her. She couldn't help being attracted to them, they were queer but lovely. Mysterious and old-fashioned with their long hair and their wide-awake hats. Beulah and Louis married young, wandering around like Adam and Eve in the garden of Eden.

Even to look at Beulah's sister, Hester Kingston now! She was well over sixty but she didn't look anything near that age. Not a wrinkle on her. She had the forehead of a twelve-year-old.

There were many people who said at the time that it was Hester who had run for help to Beulah, trying to get away from the home place. Hester seemed to be the weaker of the two, her emotions always flowing and coming out in the wrong

7

places as if she had a leak in her pipes. Like the time Nellie had said that they were out of sausages and Hester burst into tears. Or another time, when the postman remarked that it was great weather for drying and Hester flew into a fit of temper.

The postman knew full well that washing was a sensitive subject at the Kingstons. In fact he was just having a dig at Beulah and Hester couldn't stand it because she was as loyal as a dog. Many people wanted to have digs at Beulah because they felt she was ignoring them. This irritated Nellie. Could they not see Beulah was different? That she was thinking of different things? And while Nellie herself would give her right eye to know what Beulah was thinking, she disapproved of people like Danny Fox who went around trying to taunt her.

Most of the time Hester was as sweet as cake, skipping down to the Cross for messages and the chat. 'All small talk, mind,' said Sheila. 'She's as closed in her own way as Beulah. You'd never get a real bit of news out of her.'

'She's put up with a lot over the years,' said Danny, as bold as ever in the face of wrinkled-up noses.

What people did say was that it was amazing the way the twins, John and Leah had grown up and gone from primary school to secondary without a bother on them, and fair play to Leah who had gone on to the Civil Service and made a great hand of it by all accounts. Mixing with other people as if she were normal which was the one thing those children could never have been.

The Kingstons were Poleites. Poleites didn't have a church, they weren't allowed to listen to music; no gramophones, no radios, no televisions. They couldn't go to the cinema and mix with crowds. No pubs. They couldn't go to a dancehall to slide their feet over a slippery floor. They weren't allowed medical treatment. No drinking, no dancing, no doctors.

If one of them got sick, they either got better or died. No intervention. 'Dead dandy right,' said Danny Fox, agreeing

8

with the Kingstons for once, because he was notoriously tight with his money. He said that doctors were a load of money merchants. There were many people (with and without medical cards) who were inclined to agree with him and yet no one could forget Beulah's son John.

John had died in 1972 under a beech tree, three-quarters of the way up Kingston's long winding avenue. He had blood poisoning and he could just as easily have lived. Antibiotics were as common as daisies then, but forbidden to Poleites.

The worst part of it was that Beulah and Hester broke with the rules at the last moment. Hester ran to Danny Fox for brandy in the wild hope of waking John from his coma with old-style medicine. When that failed, they put him into the back of the pony-trap, hoping to get him to the hospital in time to save him.

He died before they even got to the road, his throat rattling. Stinking of the brandy which spilled down his chin, his throat, soaking the front of the spotless white shirt that they'd struggled to put over his head when they were getting ready to take him to hospital.

Chapter Two

Poleites held services in their own kitchens and parlours. Their followers came from all over the country. It was often the only way they could get couples to meet up. The girls would sit with their eyes down waiting for the nearest eligible Poleite boy to arrive, often from as far as the next province. Hester had sat for a long time with her eyes down but she never managed to get a husband. Through no fault of her own. She probably would have got one of the O'Neill twins from Bandon if they hadn't both died. Uriah, from gangrene after chicken feed got into a cut in his leg and Benjamin, from a tuberculosis.

Most of the other Poleites had been dissenters originally, so people hadn't paid much attention to their defection from the old religion. But Beulah Kingston's family had been Catholics who turned. That made the people suspicious of them. Danny Fox said that it was the devil who came to Two Mile Cross during the Land War, selling the new religion out of a tent. 'Big red eyes on him, flaming all over,' he liked to tell children if he could get any of them near enough to listen to him. 'Only the ould Protestants were taken in. *Except, of course, the Kingstons, being such bad Catholics!*'

No one paid heed to that kind of talk anymore. It was gone out with hand washing and mangles. And what's more, the younger people didn't think it was such a disgrace to run off the night your husband died. Sheila Sheehan said she had seen many such things. 'I am an experienced nurse,' ('an experienced boss', Danny Fox liked to say behind her back) 'wasn't she completely repressed? Stuck in that house all day and having to obey those weird religious laws. If she had run off with a man what about it? Maybe she wanted to enjoy herself for a change.' Sheila gave a little shudder. 'And furthermore, imagine being tied to one of those awful Poleite men with their wispy beards hanging like grass skirts from under their chins!'

Yet Sheila was a kind person and she wasn't all talk. She was passionate about modern medicine, some people believed that this passion for medicine originated from the time that John Kingston had died of blood poisoning.

'The first time she joined up at the hospital, she was only looking for a man,' Danny Fox said. 'Now since poor John Kingston died, she's gone stone out of her mind about penicillin.'

Sheila had been a wild young nurse then, going to dances and parties. She couldn't even sit still long enough to watch a film, she had no ambition to be a sister. But she heard that John was sick and figured out that he must be suffering from blood poisoning. She got hold of some antibiotics at the hospital and took them down to Kingston's a couple of days before he died. 'Ah don't go down dressed like that,' said Nellie when Sheila went off with her hair in two plaits over her ears, wearing a black and yellow plaid trouser suit. 'That loud suit! What will Beulah think?'

'John could die, you know,' Sheila said, as she went off carefully on her platform heels.

'She's like a dying wasp,' Nellie said to a customer as the two of them stood out on the road to stare after her yellow and black form tottering away under the beech trees.

Sheila waited patiently outside Beulah's back door, the stream washing over the stones as it flowed under the disused

11

water-mill. She was shy then, she had no opinions at all, only an overriding wish to save John's life. She had never even thought much about antibiotics before, only handed them out in the ward on the drugs round, thinking longingly of her tea break.

Sheila watched Beulah's face hopefully, as Beulah took the small brown glass bottle into her hand and held it up to the light. Shaking out one of the green and orange capsules onto her large creamy palm, a faint smile came across Beulah's face, before she shook herself up and handed them back to Sheila. Sheila was walking away carefully across the cobbles, defeated, when she realised that Beulah hadn't spoken one word the whole time she had been with her.

Poleites called all non-Poleites infidels, but they didn't mean it as an insult. It was just what they called them. They were careful, though, about when they used the word.

Catholics mostly referred to Poleites as Protestants. 'Pay them no heed,' the Reverend Moylan said. 'They are afraid of the power of Poleites. That is why they try to take away our name.'

After John's death, Beulah didn't think of herself as a Poleite anymore. There was no one to hold services after the death of the Reverend Moylan. As a protest at the religion that had killed John, Beulah was the first in the queue at Joe Costello's surgery for every kind of vaccination and injection and anti-biotic. Danny Fox said she was gone mad for flu jabs.

'And how does he know?' asked Nellie, getting up on her high horse. 'Since when has the likes of Danny Fox got access to Dr Costello's private notes?'

'Danny Fox hasn't got it from the horse's mouth, so don't go repeating it. I'm trying to run a business here and people have gone broke from less. If the poor creature is taking advantage of the advances of medicine, in this day and age, more luck to her. Pity she didn't do it sooner,' Nellie finished regretfully. 'Because Joe Costello has gone off an awful lot as a doctor.'

Beulah found most of the Poleite ways easier though. Radios and television were distractions and she was pleased to keep them out of the house. There was nothing wrong with sewing and reading of an evening. She still wore her long black hair twisted up in a bun. Even if she went against the rules now and had it cut, how could she possibly walk into a hairdresser's? She wouldn't know what to do, what to say, where to sit. The way hairdressers had big wide glass windows for the whole world to see her hair, all wet and plastered to her head, or whorled all round in curlers or folded into stiff tin-foil packets. Who in their right minds would want to be exposed like that? Furthermore, she'd have to stick her head into the washbasin, and how would she know that it was clean, and God knows who'd stuck their head in there before her.

She knew that people said she dyed her hair and she thought herself that it was a kind of a curse the way her hair had stayed black and youthful over the ageing face beneath it. Brushing it out at night, she stopped sometimes in front of the mirror in amazement. The blackness of it and her yellowy white face underneath, creased as an old skirt. Was this her face? And these her painful thumbs?

Hand washing had nothing to do with the pains in her hands. Why did Hester keep saying it? Why couldn't Hester leave things alone? Why couldn't she leave Beulah alone? Hadn't Beulah agreed all those years ago to start up the B&B? The greasy smell of rashers and the clatter of Hester talking to the guests. God knows what they did in the beds. No wonder Beulah had to belt the sheets against the wall when they were gone. Although they hardly ever had guests, from time to time there was the nagging fear that some might turn up. If she heard the sound of a car slowing down at the top of the drive, Beulah

13

would run up in her wellingtons and if they were strangers, take her hair down and shake it in the way she imagined mad people did. Cars speeded up again.

Beulah had always done her quiet best to discourage guests, once wearing Louis's old broad-brimmed hat and standing outside the dining-room window, making faces at a timid family from Roscommon who'd got lost on their way to the Cork–Swansea ferry. They cowered so much over their breakfast that they even irritated Hester, who had no idea of the tricks Beulah was playing behind her back.

Beulah knew her hands were as strong as ever, there was just that ache around the thumbs. She should never have told Hester about the X-ray. Now Hester wouldn't be able to stop talking about it and there was a whole week to wait for the results.

The day Beulah went to see Dr Costello, the surgery was full. She had to wait a long time but he always saw her without an appointment. She thought that she'd be full of health after going to surgery. 'Oh, that man is better than a tonic!' Nellie Sheehan used to say. 'And he's so sincere.'

Infidels often spoke about vitamin tablets and tonics and God-like doctors. Beulah listened enviously. She, too, wanted to have 'rude health' and to be 'absolutely flying' and 'full of beans'.

At first her stomach was full of a kind of a vicarious excitement that might have meant that she was full of beans, but she soon realised that it was only excitement because she was flying in the face of the Poleites. She didn't think that she could feel excitement after John's death, but she did. And after the excitement wore off, she didn't feel any better. Joe Costello grew older and greyer and more tired. She began to wonder was rude health what she had before she started going to him.

But it didn't matter how many times she went to see him, she

14

never lost the sense of anticipation. She never stopped being disappointed that he didn't pull a miracle like a soft white rabbit out of a hat.

'I've a pain in my hands. It's not arthritis, is it?'

'Sit down, Beulah.' He had less and less time to talk these days. He went straight for the drawer of the desk. Usually when Joe was busy, it was to get out his prescription pad. This time, he took a yellow form from the top drawer on the right-hand side of his desk. 'There's only one way, Beulah, to check it out and that's an X-ray. Now there's nothing to worry about in an X-ray these days.'

'No,' lied Beulah, thinking if only he touched her hands she would be cured.

'The tiniest amount of X-ray, the quarter of a blink of an eye.' He handed her the X-ray form. 'Come back in a week for the result.'

'Mind yourself, now,' he said, as she reached the door. She walked out, wondering if he would ever have the time to examine her properly again.

Beulah wondered about Joe as she plaited her hair and walked downstairs to the little scullery where a handful of broderie anglaise cloths lay soaking in Lux. She remembered him when he was young, talking about bones and muscles and blood corpuscles. It was a language forbidden to Beulah and she was drawn to Joe's words. It made his face come alive, his brown eyes burning as if there was fire behind them. A pity she couldn't have gone to him then. When he was such a fervent believer.

Beulah winced with pain, it would be too bad to have exchanged her own beliefs for some other system that was also on its way out. Beulah swished the cloths, her big hands moving in and out of the cold water. She stood for a long time, pushing the cloths through the water, until her hands grew

15

wrinkled and shrunken like a monkey's paws. When the pain grew unbearable, she began to wring out the cloths slowly and carefully.

She thought about Christmas, when she and Hester would get the ladder and take down the creaking B&B sign from the pole at the end of the lane. They would begin the baking. Puddings, cakes, pies. Hester's special porter cake. They weren't taking any guests for the month of December. Beulah had been forceful about that.

'What about the lost and desperate travellers?' asked Hester. 'They're the only ones we ever get.'

'But it's been ten years now since we've had anyone, it wouldn't kill us to help out in the season of goodwill towards all men?'

'They can drop like flies on the main road for all I care,' said Beulah. 'And isn't the family the most important of all at Christmas?'

Hester wasn't really sure what was most important at Christmas, there was no minister to ask these days and while Hester was wondering, Beulah drove her point home and won. The B&B sign was coming down. Hester agreed that there would be enough to do now with Leah and Beccy coming for Christmas.

Beulah had always looked forward to Christmas. No more greasy fry-ups and guests chatting on and on to Hester about taxation and travellers, she still remembered every dreadful detail from the last guests they had in 1987. Soon she would be taking down the curtains and sitting out in the lovely October sunshine, with a big bath of suds. An Indian summer they were having.

Hester hummed behind her, carefully disentangling tinsel and paper chains. 'We'll have to go to town for new stuff.'

Beulah thought that she would bring out her box of starch. Just the right kind of thing to be opening at Christmas time with its picture of a robin on the front of the box. She didn't use it all the year round because Nellie Sheehan had run out of starch down at the Cross and she said she couldn't get it anymore, that the wholesalers didn't have it. Beulah wondered if that was true. She liked Nellie so she hoped that she was lying.

A holly wreath hanging on the newly painted front door. The smell of ironing, three damask tablecloths, twenty-four napkins. Everything would be crisp and white like frost and snow. Everything pure and homely, grand thoughts to be having, until her thumbs twinged again and Hester's complaints about the state of the decorations became the most annoying scratchy talk that she'd ever had to endure.

Chapter Three

Beulah and Hester never mentioned to each other the possibility that Leah wouldn't turn up for Christmas at all, that she would cancel at the last moment, as she did in 1985 and 1986 and 1988. And 1990 and 1994 and two years ago in 1995. Left them high and dry with their turkeys and pickles and pies. Their Christmas cake and their plum puddings. They couldn't even bring the wasted food up to Nellie Sheehan, who was in touch with poor people, because they couldn't bear her to pity them.

Beulah and Hester didn't like this kind of food themselves so they threw the whole lot out. Carefully, late at night, in sealed bags in case Danny Fox was watching. The turkey was the worst of all, it was like trying to get rid of a murdered body.

'If we had a dog, now . . .' Hester breathed grimly as she tied yet another black bag around the lumpy parcel.

Beulah and Hester ate Denny's Irish Stew from a tin, cooked ham, fish fingers and rashers. They couldn't stand plum pudding and Christmas cake. They ate lemonade swiss roll and crunchies and their special treat was when they went to town and bought four little trifle cakes in white pleated paper cases from the confectioner's. Neither did they use damask tablecloths and starched napkins, but those, at least, weren't wasted, they could be used again.

Beulah and Hester agreed that it was the expense that was galling, that they didn't really mind, even though they had been dying to see Beccy. Especially after all the interesting snippets that Leah had been dropping over the phone; 'No, her hair is gone dark, yes like a raven and very long. I think she'll go in for science, but they tell me she's very fond of religion too, isn't that unusual for someone nowadays? She's learning the flute, she won three medals for Irish dancing. She's reading George Eliot.'

'Leah would never trick us again, would she?' Beulah asked, the morning of her X-ray appointment, when the two of them sat beside the range drinking tea, custard creams lying ignored on the plate.

'Leah was never like that, she was never a blackguard,' Hester said. 'She must have her own troubles.'

'What troubles could she possibly have with her grand job and her daughter grown up?' Beulah snapped. 'Beccy is eighteen and we haven't seen her since she was three. She might as well be in Australia!'

Leah had always been difficult. She had resented Beulah's attentions to John. Beulah hadn't known at the time. If Leah could have come out straight with it instead of hanging around with Hester and making it look like she preferred Hester and didn't care too much about Beulah. If only she hadn't waited until after John's death.

'It's too late, now, Mama,' she said, when Beulah put her hand out beside the coffin.

'Young people can be cruel,' Hester said. 'Give her time.'

But Beulah knew only too well about young people. Hadn't she been one herself once? A young cruel person. And always paying the price when it was too late. She didn't want it to be too late for Leah. But she was far too proud to plead again.

'You have to try harder,' said Hester. 'Don't you know that she's as proud as yourself?'

19

'And doesn't that mean that it's only useless to be trying at all?'

'Beulah, she hasn't just lost her brother, she has lost her twin. You know John was a big part of Leah.'

'Isn't it funny now that Beccy likes religion,' said Hester.

'Ah, it's not the same thing as being religious, though. I would say that Beccy has a studious interest, the same as her father had. She would like to be examining us now like insects or something. There's a lot of people like that around nowadays, and they're mostly looking for faults. The infidels get a lot of them, Nellie Sheehan told me, going round trying to embarrass everyone.'

'Well, infidels have a lot to be embarrassed about,' sniffed Hester. 'What about the way we were treated in school?'

Beulah didn't bother to answer. She knew Hester well enough to know that she'd run a mile from any kind of an investigation. She was thinking about Leah's husband, Peter. Leah pushed Beulah away at John's funeral. She said that Peter was her only support. She only said it to hurt her, Beulah knew that and Hester said so. As if a twenty-six-year-old girl as determined as Leah wasn't capable of picking up her bags and going off to Dublin on her own. 'You never held my hand when we were walking over Patrick's bridge,' said Leah, 'and I was terrified that I'd fall between the pillars into the Lee. You always held John's hand, though. Too much, I'd say.'

Peter was red in the face with embarrassment and pity as he took Leah outside before John's body was confined. He squeezed Beulah's arm and drove carefully away. He was quiet and he didn't say much but he was very good to Leah. When Peter died of cancer, Leah kept saying that she had lost her best friend. He was a friend to Beulah too and perhaps that was why it was after his death that Leah stopped visiting.

'Wasn't it strange, too, that Peter got lung cancer when he

20

was so careful?' Hester said to Beulah, reading her mind the way she often did.

'Getting cancer is not a form of carelessness,' said Beulah. 'And he was not a sinner, either. Dr Costello says that the whole country would be jumping with health only for the cigarettes.'

'Hannah and Bertie wouldn't have allowed the marriage,' insisted Hester. 'They would have checked him out. Wasn't he related to the O'Neills? Do you remember Uriah O'Neill and the chicken feed and the gangrene?' her voice trembled.

'What has that got to do with anything?' Beulah tried to be kind, she knew that Hester was still disappointed about losing both the O'Neill twins. 'Gangrene and lung cancer are not related, I don't think anyway.'

'Cigarettes are the worst of all,' she added more firmly.

How could she have known that Leah had wanted more care? Hadn't Leah stood up for herself, hadn't she given the master a black eye the day he tried to push her around the classroom like he had done to generations before her. It was the talk of the village. Beulah wouldn't have known if Nellie Sheehan hadn't congratulated Leah in front of a big crowd in the shop.

'The only one to beat that old blackguard,' said Nellie, handing out a big bag of Emerald toffees to Leah.

Everyone in the shop had been taught by Master Reilly and they formed a ring around the counter, all wanting to talk about him. It was like a convention. Beulah couldn't understand why they wanted to remember all the vivid details. She tried to usher Leah out, but the crowd were having none of it. Martin Dunne was talking about the time Master Reilly had tied Frank Taylor to a tree for eight hours and he fainted clean away and had to be carried off by his mother in the evening like Mary recovering Jesus's body from the centurions. The time he had locked small Pat Murphy into his cupboard. The sharpness of

21

the creases on his trousers, the dead straight lines on his face, the cruelty that went on and on. Even the good people got at least four slaps a day.

'Ah, lads, why?' asked Nellie and she wasn't looking for an answer.

'Because,' Danny Fox was in like a shot, 'he fecking enjoyed it.'

'Language, Danny!' thundered Nellie.

'And no one challenged him,' Danny went on as he rolled up his sleeve. 'I've scars, do you want to see them?' he bent down to Leah.

'Yuch,' said Leah and pushed her way out of the shop, with Beulah hurrying along behind her. As the door jangled shut, she could just make out Nellie moaning at Danny, 'Why oh why do you have to ruin every good conversation?'

Leah opened the bag of Emerald's straight away and began to chew fast as if her life depended on it.

'Did you really hit Master Reilly?'

Leah wouldn't look at Beulah, she kept chewing and looking straight ahead. 'It was a mistake, I put my hand up to protect myself. He had never pushed me around before and I'd seen the others putting their hands up before. But I must have done it too hard. He got an awful fright and fell back. He thought I meant it, his eye was red and pink and purple nearly straight away. It was then that I gave him a black look so that he'd think I did it on purpose. He hasn't been near me since Tuesday.' Leah unwrapped another Emerald and shoved it into her mouth before she finished chewing the first one. 'Haven't you noticed how long the nails have grown on my right hand? I can't cut them with my left hand.'

Beulah didn't know what to make of that. All she could think was that she was dying for an Emerald, the scent of vanilla and chocolate drifted on the wind but Leah never offered.

Now, of course she realised what Leah was trying to say. She wanted Beulah to cut her nails and notice her hair and maybe a

22

dozen other things that Beulah couldn't have realised when Leah seemed so independent. John always asked for help. But maybe she had been more interested and ready to help him anyway. John, in Beulah's eyes, was a small Louis, another chance, How could Beulah have known that Leah wanted her hand held going over Patrick's bridge? It was John's soft hand she remembered sliding into her fist. His shiny brown hair falling to one side like a brown beret. All she had wanted to do was to keep John alive and a boy forever, with short pants and no beard.

Chapter Four

Beulah drove up to the county hospital, Monday afternoon, an hour before her appointment. A cautious driver, she had learned to drive late in life, after John's death, around the same time she had taken up with medicine. But she still felt that her car was a kind of mechanical pony. She worried that it would not be able to make the steep hill, that it would slip down. She was afraid to take her hand off the steering wheel to change gears and the car roared in pain as she pressed hard on the accelerator. She murmured to it, 'Come on, now,' and it climbed the long winding road to the hospital.

Down below, the river ran its blueish stream between the golds and reds and the evergreens. It made her dizzy to look at it. When Beulah arrived on the level ground of the hospital car park, she noticed that her hands were wet with perspiration. She pulled into a space quickly, turned the engine off and at the same time bent over to get a tissue out of the glove box. The car gave a sudden buck. Trembling, Beulah put the gearstick into neutral and grasped handfuls of tissues, wiping her face and hands. She looked around the car park then and checked in the rear mirror, luckily no one was watching. She was always afraid that the car might be taken off her for dangerous driving.

Beulah sat for a long time in the car park, rubbing her

thumbs, the sun beating warm through the glass on her face. The Reverend Moylan would turn in his grave at the thought of a Poleite having an X-ray. Not that she thought she was a Poleite anymore. Had she ever known what a Poleite was, she wondered.

When Hester and Beulah were growing up, sometimes it felt like everything apart from breathing was forbidden. Once Hester asked the Reverend Moylan was it all right to go into the chemist's to buy a bandage. He stared down at Hester and Beulah with his eyebrows quivering for a moment, then shepherded them into the parlour. He sat them down together on a sofa and stood over them, swaying from side to side, his hands buried somewhere deep in his black pockets, trying to give himself a casual air.

'Don't be frightened, Hester. You did well to ask. I like openness. There is nothing wrong with bandages at all, but you have no need to buy bandages, doesn't your good mother make her own? Chemist shops are dens of iniquity. Packed bursting with drugs, opiums and bromides, abominations of God's holy earth that he made with his own hands. Not to mention the shelves of paint and powder for poor women who don't know any better.'

His blue eyes glittered at Hester kindly, 'Do you understand what it is to be a Poleite at all? Do you know why we're here? Why God sent us?'

Hester's head wavered nervously between a nod and a shake. Beulah didn't move. The Reverend Moylan said, 'The Poleites were founded by the great Samuel Pole during the reign of Queen Victoria. He saw the way the world was hurtling towards destruction with its factories and science. Its sinful materialism, love of luxury and pleasure. He saw the pain it was causing God's earth, God was crying out to him in pain every night in his sleep.' The Reverend stretched out his long black arms in a plaintive gesture. Beulah could sense that Hester's

25

body was rigid with fear as she sat beside her. She got an uncomfortable urge to laugh.

'Above all,' the Reverend's voice went low and dramatic, 'Samuel Pole saw the rise of doctors, the dissections and vaccinations, the interfering with God's will, and he broke away from his Anglican faith. "Back to King James's Bible," he said, "and back to producing your own provisions on your own farms. Away from material things and vanities for women. Away from the factories with their devilish machines, away from all machines and cities, the loud music, the bright lights, and above all away from the mad scientists and doctors, drunk with their own power, with their jars and their Bunsen burners and needles!" '

The Reverend stopped to take breath. 'And so the Poleites became self-sufficent and they rejected modern medicine. They knew that doctors were only death spreaders and chancers. They kept far away from hospitals and chemist shops, from towns and sinful pleasure. They accepted God's will and did not fight death. *The Lord giveth and the Lord taken away.* Amen.'

Beulah smiled as she remembered that afternoon so long ago. Poleites didn't follow Samuel Pole's teachings to the letter. Some farmers bought machines like tractors during the thirties. They weren't completely self-sufficent; they bought certain commodities that they couldn't grow like tea and sugar, but they dressed modestly, led austere lives and above all kept away from doctors. Beulah looked at her watch. Ten minutes to two o'clock. She put on her gloves and got out of the car.

'Is that Beulah?' she was dismayed to hear Sheila Sheehan calling out to her as she came across from the other side of the park. She bore down on Beulah like a gander moving in for the attack. If Beulah had known how to swear, she might have sworn. Instead she stopped. 'I thought you worked in the Regional?'

26

'I'm down giving a talk to the nurses inside. I'm in health education now.'

Beulah looked Sheila up and down, her jeans and runners. Her short hair. Where had all the beautiful white starch and veils gone? As a child all she had wanted was a nurse's outfit. Sometimes she wanted a white dress. Sometimes a blue and white striped one. The first-aid kit with the red cross, the upside-down watch. The square hat sitting on top of a french roll.

Years ago, Margaret Costello, the doctor's daughter, got a nurse's kit. When no one had even heard of them. It arrived in a brown parcel from London. The postman told the Kingstons all about it. And then Margaret Costello brought it to school one day. She showed it to certain chosen girls, but Beulah had caught a glimpse during the Angelus, when Margaret's satchel fell on its side.

All the other children stood up to say the Angelus, but Beulah and Hester would remain sitting, staring into space, putting on distant expressions. Once Hester had joined in absent-mindedly and Beulah caught the flesh of her upper arm in a vicious pinch. There was a bow-shaped bruise on Hester's arm for weeks.

Beulah felt bad but she didn't let on. 'That'll teach you,' she said, adding, 'and isn't it a fierce ugly colour?'

'Look polite but do not look impressed,' their father told them. *An angel of the Lord declared unto Mary*. Beulah could see the dress. Blue and white. Crisp. Stripes. A little bit of red tape or ribbon, she craned her neck to try to make it out. Master Reilly's thin lips were mouthing the Angelus, he never looked at the Kingstons during the Angelus. Usually the Kingstons looked away, too, but this time Beulah wanted to make sure that no one could see her looking at the nurse's outfit. Sometimes, if the master couldn't see them, the other children stared at the Kingstons. As if they expected them to have fits at the

27

sound of the prayers. Once, by mistake, Beulah had caught Danny Fox's eye and he'd winked at her. But Beulah was never caught like that again, she pinched herself in fury all the way home.

Beulah wanted to take the nurse's outfit out of Margaret Costello's bag and hold it against herself. She had heard the others saying that there was a short cape as well, made of navy-blue felt. How short? Beulah checked Hester to make sure that her mind wasn't wandering again.

Two weeks later, Margaret Costello had gone away to boarding school and the chosen girls remarked with satisfaction that she wouldn't be able to take her nursing outfit with her.

Then one day Beulah got more than a glimpse.

'Is Hester not enough for you?' her mother cried out, the awful evening that they found out she'd been playing with the doctor's son, Joe Costello.

He had come home from boarding school. Beulah was in her last year at primary school. She met him when she was coming back from the shop with a strong brown bag full of sugar. She'd been wetting her finger and dipping it in the sugar, sucking and sucking a sweetness that made her heart pound and legs tremble with energy. After a while she looked into the bag and panicked when she noticed the soggy crests her moist fingers had made in the sugar.

Apart from the fact that it was during the war years and sugar was rationed, Poleites came down hard on greed. Sugar had come very near to being banned on more than one occasion. Beulah's little finger was dry, she began to scrabble away at the hard cliffs of ruined sugar. Nothing for it but to eat those bits as well. The sugar bag was getting lighter. A wet patch on the side began to tear. Beulah walked in circles, around the entrance to Kingston's leafy avenue.

Joe came along, carrying a football under his arm. He had

28

turf-brown hair and two half crowns in his pocket. He treated her as if she was an ordinary person. As he walked her down to the Cross, the sky seemed lower, the tree trunks blacker. Against her ear drums there was a muffled beating like waves on a sea shore. Beulah had never been to the sea but she had listened to the sounds from a pale shell that Louis Kingston kept in his hay barn.

Beulah waited outside the shop while Joe bought another bag of sugar from Nellie Sheehan's mother. She could see the shiny shovel-shaped scoop in Old Maggie Sheehan's hand as she held it in the air, her face lit up with questions and Joe answering away.

When Joe came out, he told her that Mrs Sheehan always had a bit extra for the people she liked, but they were to tell nobody in case there was an outbreak of jealousy. People might say that she wasn't being fair with the rations and the government would be down on top of her.

Joe asked Beulah to stand in goal while he kicked the ball through her long feet. Then he invited her into the drawing room and told her to lie down on the floor.

'I need to listen to your heart.' His eyes were flecked with gold in the sunlight. 'I'll cast light into your darkness.' He said it like a Poleite minister would. Beulah lay on the doctor's creamy carpet, waiting for the touch of his fingers. She wanted to be cured of something even though she had no idea of what it might be. Catholics seemed to have many ways of starting all over again. Cures and miracles and confessions.

Miss Foot, the junior teacher, had gone into raptures with the First Communion class, about the shine of a soul coming out from a good confession. Beulah was in the corner learning her tables, but she couldn't help listening to Miss Foot's urgent stage whispers, 'Oh, white beyond white and see-through, oh no one can know how clear until we're all up there above the clouds, oh matchless!' Judging by the furtive glances which

Miss Foot was casting at her, it was clear that she thought that Beulah was missing out on something good. Beulah lay on Costello's carpet, full of longing for purity and cures.

'Sit up a minute,' Joe said, then. 'This is my sister's,' he held out the small blue and white stripy uniform. Beulah stared at it for a minute, so small and wrinkled that at first she could hardly believe it was the same grand outfit Margaret had been showing all her friends. 'Put it on, will you!' he said, impatiently. It was tight and Beulah could hardly get it over the sleeves of her grey woollen dress. She was big for her age but small compared to what she became after, and she was very proud to be wearing that dress. It might not be as well ironed as she remembered, but it still made her feel beautiful.

Beulah lay down again and he unbuttoned the uniform and her long grey dress underneath until he had exposed a tiny bit of her upper chest. He swung out his father's stethoscope and placed its chilliness against her skin. 'I'll cure you,' he said and Beulah shivered.

Ever since that moment, Beulah thought that hospitals must be very very cool places. Like ice houses. Her father, Bertie Kingston, had told her about the ice house he'd seen on the O'Neills' estate when he was a child. Too cold for germs to live, he said. The Kingstons talked a lot about germs, as did all Poleites. Without doctors, they knew that germs could kill them. 'But you can pick them up in hospitals, too,' Bertie Kingston kept reminding them. 'Germs are hardy out,' he said, so often that Beulah thought he admired them really.

Staring at Joe's dark red lips and thinking of ice houses, Beulah heard none of the sounds that should have warned her, neither did Joe. Like Beulah, he jumped when he heard, 'Daddy, Joe's got one of those Protestants down on the floor inside!'

'A Poleite, you mean,' said the mother, peering over Margaret's shoulder, identifying Beulah's creed in the same cool way that Bertie Kingston would identify the breed of a dog. 'A little greyhound, by Jove. Ah, what a grand little head on that springer spaniel, is he a good setter?' Only Mrs Costello's face wasn't full of love the way Bertie's was when he looked at the dogs. She wasn't admiring the shape of Beulah's head or any other part of her. She was not admiring Beulah at all.

Dr Costello was kind, but distant. He kept well back behind himself. Beulah could see that her presence was a trouble to him. Both husband and wife couldn't get her out quick enough.

'Your mother would die if she knew,' Rita Costello kept saying.

Knew what? The doctor wheeled around his big car and Beulah felt tiny for once, sitting in the back seat, Rita Costello with her dyed short hair and perfume and earrings, talking about shame and mortification. Strange. What was bothering Rita Costello, who wore her sins of vanity as if they were the height of respectability?

But no longer strange. People wore anything these days. In the grounds of the county hospital, fifty-seven years later, Beulah looked at Sheila's jeans. How could she possibly be comfortable, laced in with all those hard zips and studs and buckles?

Sheila took the appointment card out of Beulah's hand, 'Do you know where X-ray is? Don't go in the main entrance. Go round the side of the new extension and up the steps. You're a bit early, you know that. Mrs Treadle will be out shopping still.'

Beulah retrieved the card from Sheila. Of course she knew where the X-ray Department was. She had been doing her research for the last week, dropping a question here and there to Nellie Sheehan, suffering all the digressions about Nellie's knee replacements and her pre-op chest X-rays. Operation! She didn't think that it would go that far. It would never go that far, surely.

As Beulah neared the X-ray building, she looked back,

31

expecting to see Sheila still looking after her, but the grounds were empty, apart from a physiotherapist guiding an S-shaped old woman along the paths between the lawns. She winced at the sight and felt deserted. As if she missed Sheila when she knew that she really didn't.

Beulah climbed the steps and rang the bell. It didn't seem to be working. She had thought that Mrs Treadle would have had some kind of assistant to hold the fort while she was out shopping. She pushed the door and it gave way into a large waiting area with plants and magazines and a fish tank. Beulah didn't like fish. She sat down with her back to them and folded her arms. There were underlined notices in bouncy black handwriting all over the wall.

RING THE BELL ONCE AND ONCE ONLY.
X-RAY BY APPOINTMENT ONLY.
RESULTS TAKE ONE WEEK DO NOT ASK THE RADIOGRAPHER FOR PREVIEWS.
SHE CANNOT TAKE RESPONSIBILITY FOR ANY DIAGNOSIS.

A grey square door with yellow and black symbols painted on it. *Radiation. Keep out! Authorised personnel only.*

What would her father have thought if he could have have lived to see her with her skirt a good two inches above her ankles, wearing a bright blue cardigan and sitting in the softest armchair in the X-ray Department of the county hospital.

Bertie Kingston believed that X-rays were evil, and when the news of Hiroshima and Nagasaki was announced, he said that he wasn't one bit surprised. He deplored the amount of X-rays that went on in hospitals. 'Do they honestly think that they will be able to eradicate tuberculosis?' Bertie and a good many other Poleites expected the whole nation to burn themselves out with X-rays, leaving the green and lovely countryside free for the holy tribe of Poleites. The minister had thought so too.

He'd thundered out his sermon in Kingston's parlour, 'Mass X-ray vans parked in every village like armoured tanks in an occupied country. They'll see, oh they will, the pagans, there's worse things on earth than a bit of tuberculosis.' Reverend Moylan shook inside his black loose suit, 'Poisonous arrows flung by women in white coats, wearing high heels!'

Beulah looked down at her big beige shoes. She wished her hands would stop shaking. To calm herself, she tried to remember what a Poleite man looked like. It was so long since she had seen one. Poleites weren't allowed to take photographs and even the few Poleite men she'd come across in recent years had abandoned the old styles.

John had been the last one that she had known. John had pale skin like all the other Poleite men. They had pale skin from wearing those wide-brimmed hats that fended off every scrap of sunlight. Then the hair pressed down and cut bowl-shaped. Beulah imagined that a handsome man would look appealing like that, a shiny petal of hair over his eyes, but she'd never seen a handsome Poleite. They went bald fast for some reason. It could have been a hereditary thing as most Poleites were interbred. Poor John receded at fifteen, that was why he took to wearing the hat, when more and more of the young Poleites were giving them up. It was not that he'd gone all orthodox like people said.

But even a handsome man could hardly hold his own with that glibby long beard growing in a half circle under his chin. The Poleite beard made them all look like greedy, cruel, Chinese emperors, when the poor creatures were only gauche and shy.

They blushed little red carnations into their pale cheeks if a woman even looked at them. Sam Potts had a weakness in a Bandon café when a waitress asked, 'Was it a pot of tea for two, love?'

33

'She called me *love*,' he kept saying to his wife as they drove home in the pony and trap.

He took to walking past the café. It was whispered that he was consumed with a passion. That a middle-aged woman with dyed blonde hair, 'a common tramp of a waitress', Beulah heard her mother saying, was stalking his dreams. Sam Potts maintained that he was only making sure she *wasn't* there before daring to enter. 'I've got a terrible thirst upon me for tea.'

Deborah Potts took advice from the Reverend and Sam Potts was told to stay away from the town of Bandon and all cafés.

But, because they were shy didn't mean that they weren't the most stubborn creatures on earth. Beulah thought of her husband, Louis Kingston. They had the same surname, although they came from different stock. 'We must have been the one crowd, once, if you could go back far enough,' Louis had said proudly the day they drove home from their wedding.

The bang of another door behind the grey door made Beulah sit upright. Footsteps and slamming of heavy objects. There was the sound of switches being thrown. Any minute now Mrs Treadle would come out in her high heels and fork Beulah into the glowing flames of the X-ray machine. 'Roentgen has a lot to answer for,' Bertie Kingston had said, although Reverend Moylan had been kinder. 'The man should have known better but the poor soul couldn't have known what he was letting himself in for when he was putty melting in the red hot hands of the devil.'

34

Chapter Five

Could her conversion to medicine after John's death have led to all of this? Beulah listened to the crashing and buzzing of machines starting up. The pain, the painkillers, the trips up and down to Joe Costello's surgery, now the X-rays. She'd got the idea of arthritis from going to his surgery in the first place and sitting too close to dependent cripples.

Reverend Moylan would have thought so, 'Once they have a hold of you, oh the game is up! It doesn't matter who they are. Quacks or professors. They reel you in until you're floundering away with your mouth open like a fish gasping for life.'

Would she end up smelling like those old people who were too weak to wash themselves? Who roared with pain and embarrassment from lonely farmhouses when the district nurse came out manhandling them into baths? Beulah sat listening to the clicking of switches and then there was a great splash that seemed to come from inside a big container, as if Mrs Treadle was churning butter.

The door opened. Mrs Treadle was blonde and wore jewellery. Her resemblance to Joe Costello's mother was incredible. But then she was Joe Costello's young cousin. Her white uniform was clenched at the waist by a thick green belt two inches wide. Clipped onto her belt was an array of objects, steel clips marked with R and L, felt-tip pens, a couple of biros, a tape measure.

'Mrs Beulah Kingston!'

Beulah nodded briefly. If Mrs Treadle thought that she was going to plead for quick results or stagger into the room holding onto her arm, she was in for a surprise. Beulah rose to her full height of six feet and began to button up her cardigan carefully.

'No need for that, Mrs Kingston,' said Mrs Treadle, gripping Beulah firmly by the elbow and leading her determinedly into the room. Beulah tried to disengage her arm but Mrs Treadle had a tight grip and was pulling Beulah so fast towards the X-ray room, it was hopeless.

'Which knee is it? Is it the left? Mrs Kingston, I hate rushing people, now but are you wearing tights or stockings? If we need to do your hips as well then we'll have to get your girdle off. Of course the doctors won't tell you these things but there's no need to be embarrassed with me.'

Beulah winced at the mention of embarrassment, so Mrs Treadle knew all about Beulah and that she was a Poleite. 'The weird modesty of the Poleites,' Joe Costello had said to her face only a few years ago. But she could hardly tell Joe about the real reason she had gone red when he rolled up her sleeve for the injection. It was the feel of his fingers on the soft skin of her wrist.

And even if she did have a weird modesty, she still couldn't see why she had to take off so many clothes for an X-ray of her thumbs.

'It's my thumbs,' she protested.

A dusty blush went over Mrs Treadle's face, 'I thought that it was your back. How did I make that out now?' She peered at the yellow form in a short-sighted way, 'You are right, though. It is definitely hands.' As the blush faded, Mrs Treadle put on a stern look. 'You know there's far too much work here for one person. I'm like a little pony trotting up and down the hospital all day.' Beulah was embarrassed at this outburst, she looked at Mrs Treadle's black shiny shoes. She wanted to get out as quickly as possible. She didn't want to hear Mrs Treadle comparing herself to a pony. It made her feel like a hairy-legged dray horse.

'Now, let us look at what he's written anyway. Query arthritis. A.P. thumbs. Where does Joe think he's going?'

'It's just my thumbs.'

'You'll need both hands and the two views. P.A. and ball catchers.'

'It's just my thumbs,' Beulah looked fearfully at the big ugly X-ray machine.

'Look, it's for arthritis, you have to have the whole of the hands.'

'It's not arthritis. We don't know yet.'

'Well, what else do you think it is, at your age? Let's face it, Beulah. Put your hands down here.' At the same time as she pressed Beulah into a seat, Mrs Treadle pushed a steel plate under Beulah's long hands and flattened them down firmly. 'What age are you now? Let me see, 1927, you're seventy. I'd consider myself lucky if I were you. A bit of a pain in your thumb! There was a woman in here the other day, forty-two years of age and she's in a wheelchair. She has to take four different kinds of tablets before she's able to sit up and drink her tea of a morning.'

'What's lucky?' Beulah asked, as Mrs Treadle opened her fingers out and arranged them on the plate.

Mrs Treadle didn't answer.

Beulah's hands were as dry and as crisp as brown paper bags. The skin crackled when Mrs Treadle touched it. Beulah looked at her thumbs as if from a great distance, there was no pain now. Maybe there was still time to stop and walk out. Forget the whole thing and maybe the pain might never come back. It was hard to remember what the pain had been like, an hour ago.

The buzzer went in the waiting room, it went again and again and again. Beulah jumped every time.

37

'I've learned to ignore it,' said Mrs Treadle. 'They can read the signs, they're only trying to make me jump faster and that I cannot do.'

Mrs Treadle's touch was surprisingly light. A restful tingling went up Beulah's arm. She almost closed her eyes, wanting to fall asleep. The cool impersonal touch released a wave of memory and longing.

She was reeled in and there was no point in fighting it. She had started it, years before. All because she wanted to be touched in a different way. At night, under the mill when it was still turning. The water dripping and clear, falling from the wooden slats of the wheel. The thunderous hypnotic noise by the side of the house before it ran into the whitewashed trough outside Kingston's scullery.

All because she wanted to learn the names of all the bones. The strength of her hands then, and now it was gone. She had arthritis, Mrs Treadle was right. What else could it possibly be? Her punishment had been a long time coming while she was keeping her house spotless and shining with Fairy Snow and Flash. Cleanliness is next to godliness and surely very near to hospitals.

Bertie Kingston called hospitals germ factories, but there was nothing whiter than the habit of a nursing nun who'd come to the school all those years ago. Vaccinations in the cold classroom. A line of children with their sleeves rolled up, leaning hard against the desks because they couldn't trust their trembling legs to stand up on their own. Miss Foot, the teacher, had given the Kingstons pitying looks but it was the children in the lumpy waiting line that Beulah felt sorry for.

Mrs Treadle rolled the big X-ray machine across the room. It rumbled as it came, dragging thick snaky cables with it. As Mrs Treadle turned a knob on the machine, a ticking noise started and a square of light illuminated Beulah's hands where they lay on the steel plate. A black cross divided the square of light.

Beulah craned her neck looking up into the X-ray tube. She could make out a mirror and various shutters and doors, like some kind of a puzzle. Mrs Treadle gently pushed Beulah's head away, 'Mind yourself now. There's nothing at all interesting up there.' Mrs Treadle took a breath in, 'Oh, I forgot your ring, if you can manage to take it off. Your watch too. I like to get the wrists in as well. It is important for arthritis.'

Mrs Treadle jumped at a beeping noise that started going somewhere behind the big control panel. 'You'll have to excuse me now, for a moment, while I put developer in the chemical mixer. I'm completely on my own, you know. There will be a serious accident here, one of these days. Someone is going to fall off that big high table and they'll only have themselves to blame.'

Beulah wondered who *they* were. The people who were going to fall off the big high table or the people who had left Mrs Treadle to work on her own. Beulah had never taken off her wedding ring before. She married at seventeen before she stopped growing and by now the gold band was well embedded. She held her breath, pulled and pushed while, in the backround, Mrs Treadle continued to shout sorry to the accompaniment of swishing noises beyond the control panel. Another beeping noise started up, 'Now we're out of fixer! I'm going to have to leave you while I go down to the theatre darkroom to get some more. I won't be long.' Mrs Treadle's heels went into the distance.

Beulah held her breath, she pulled and pulled. She bit the insides of her cheeks with frustration. Her hand was swelled up like a prize marrow. Why did Mrs Treadle want to X-ray her whole hand when it was only her thumbs? There was a searing pain in her ring finger. She would have arthritis *there* next. The whole thing was going to spread and twist her body into a crippled hoop. There would be no more washing. No more shining house with white curtains blowing.

The room began to grow dark. Louis's face swam up. She thought that she was dying, going into darkness until she realised that the ticking noise had stopped in the X-ray tube and it was the absence of the square light-beam that made the room grow dark.

But Louis's face did not go away, it bobbed in the darkness. Disembodied. Just the long fringe of his beard floating underneath, like a cover for a mysterious hand that was moving his puppet head.

'Go away,' Beulah said to the head. 'You've no right to come up here to the county hospital. *You're* a Poleite.'

The head said nothing, it came closer and opened its mouth wide into a long yawning tunnel with wispy beard flying back around it. Beulah found herself sliding down the tunnel, head first and landing at the bottom, her mouth full of earth.

The match had been made between herself and Louis one Sunday afternoon in her parent's house. There was homemade lemonade and layered coffee cake. Han had been saving the sugar coupons for months, managing to stock up enough despite Beulah's raids on the pantry. Reverend Moylan beaming. Bertie Kingston's face not happy, just relieved.

Bertie kept filling up the glasses of lemonade, his beard covered in coffee-cake crumbs. He wolfed slice after slice with the relief of getting Beulah settled. It was not greed, Bertie knew that much. He was just relieved, he'd seen infidels drink like that after getting a bad fright. A near accident during the harvest. Bertie knew many infidels, all religions pitched in together to save the hay, they were not bad men and one or two could work nearly as hard as a Poleite.

But Reverend Moylan had his eye on Bertie, he could hear his excited breathing. He pushed the coffee cake right down to the other end of the table with his lanky black-clothed arm and said. 'You've had enough, now.'

40

'You're right, there,' said Bertie, agreeing. 'I wasn't aware of myself, I'm that happy to see Beulah settled and safe.'

He looked at Beulah, he touched her long thin arm. She had hair like the wing of a blackbird. He knew even though he wasn't supposed to know, that it came down to her knees. Saturday nights, they all washed their hair and Beulah's was so slow to dry. Impatient at being cooped up in the bedroom, she had often hung it out the window to dry. Coming up from the paddock and seeing the black sheet out the window, it had made him think of death and unlucky things. But coming closer, he'd seen how it shone and the softness of it, under the hard shine of the stars. He had wanted to climb up it. Now if that was how he, Bertie, felt, what would an ordinary infidel feel? What would he do? Most likely wind her hair around his arm and run off with her.

Beulah had two big brown eyes, her eyelashes were as long as a Friesian's and her skin was the colour of butter from an old-fashioned dairy. Bertie wasn't saying any of this to Reverend Moylan. Let the Reverend think that he was greedy. Coffee cake wasn't on his mind, all he wanted was to keep Beulah safe. Sitting there in her grey dress with the pearl grey collar. Her thick black stockings only setting off her two thin ankles peeping above her black shoes. The big coil of hair at her long neck. She was a beautiful giraffe. Her creamy cheek. He could see the tiny muscles flexing in her face as she chewed cake.

Beulah chewed the cake automatically. Louis Kingston was trying to look at her out of the corner of his eye. That eye glinted as he pretended to blink innocently under the watchful gaze of the Reverend. Louis's Poleite beard was a reddish down, straggly. His hat brim came to the top of his eyes, he was most sinister looking. Two bright red spots glowed on his cheeks and the lily white skin on his face was not related to his dark work-cracked hands. Those work-cracked hands edged towards the

41

old Ludo box that Beulah's mother, Han, had laid out on the table earlier.

'You'll probably want to play a game together,' she said, as if Beulah was happy to play shyly with her future husband. Louis's seamed hands kept advancing towards the Ludo box, he was trying to meet Beulah's eye. He couldn't wait to start rolling the dice. Ludo was the nearest a Poleite ever got to gambling and the Reverend wasn't completely happy about them playing it.

Beulah had never been safe from the day she had lain on the floor of Costello's drawing room while Joe had listened to her heart with the cold shining stethoscope. And she mightn't even have been safe before that. Hadn't she been gorging herself on sugar and going round and round the top of Kingston's avenue like a girl willing the devil to turn up? And hadn't the devil arrived right on cue with a football under his arm?

Han Kingston knew what Bertie thought of Beulah, but as far as Han herself was concerned, Beulah was a big long yoke of an ox-eyed girl and it had always been troublesome to get clothes to fit her. Han was no judge of beauty. She didn't know about such things. All she knew was that Beulah hated the height of herself, loved sugar too much and was not a devout Poleite. Now, Hester was dying for a Poleite husband. Hester craved sour things, crab apples, pickles, even vinegar straight from the bottle.

And the Reverend Moylan thought that it was only sugar that was dangerous, 'Gives you a straight slide down into greed,' he barked often enough in their parlour.

Han wondered what he would say if he saw the way Hester drank vinegar as if it was intoxicating wine. And the way she couldn't get enough of sucking lemons since Beulah's marriage had been announced. This very morning Han had caught her rummaging in the bins, looking for the empty lemon halves that

42

had been used to make the lemonade. As far as Han knew, it wasn't downright dangerous like the habit of eating paint that some children had, but it couldn't be healthy for the body, not to mention the soul.

As Poleite boys went, Louis Kingston was a catch. Young, strong, big farm. No history of illness in the family. Not like those handsome O'Neill twins. Hester lost both of them before they'd even begun, but Han had always thought that the O'Neills were a bad bet anyway. They had bad chests, their house had always been full of TB. Han tried to tell Hester that she was lucky really. It would be worse to be widowed with young children later, when whichever O'Neill she had married would inherit his consumption. But poor Hester couldn't see it that way. Han didn't know which daughter was worse off, the one who ate sugar or the one who sucked lemons.

They finished up the lemonade and the Reverend had two more slices of cake. 'I'll remove the temptation,' he said and curled his dainty white fingers tight around his green and white china plate so as not to drop the crumbs. Beulah and Hester took the crumbs out to the birds later and stayed in the yard talking while Han washed the china carefully and the men went into the parlour to get ready for service.

King James's Bible was of prime importance to Poleites. The impossibility of carrying out Samuel Pole's teaching to the absolute letter made them long for structure. The Bible provided the necessary backbone. Service consisted mostly of the Old Testament and the Reverend Moylan's passionate reciting of the psalms. He was uncomfortable with music. The Reverend had a habit of swaying when he heard a hymn. He couldn't help himself and it seemed dangerously close to dancing so he cut the hymns out of his service altogether. Every minister interpreted Samuel Pole differently, but they all went for austerity.

Beulah glared at Hester under the lilac tree. She picked

43

blossoms and crushed them between her thumb and finger, 'I'll do what I like with lilac, don't you talk to me when I'm doing my duty enough as it is.'

'It wouldn't be duty to me.' Hester pulled her fair hair tighter into its bun.

'Did you see that kind of nasty glint in his eyes?'

'What's wrong with you? Can't you see how fond he is of you! You're so lucky.'

Reverend Moylan was intoning *The Lord is my shepherd*. The beautiful words sailed like paper planes out of the parlour window . . . *through pastures green* . . . *beside running water . . . he leadeth me*. Beulah thought of Joe Costello. His soft white hands. He told her the week before that he wanted to be a surgeon, but his father wouldn't let him. Until he said that, Beulah had thought that a GP and a surgeon were one and the same thing. The older Poleites had spoken about Joe's father as if he was ripping out gall bladders and sewing up ulcers in his surgery every day of the week. But why was it called the surgery then? That would have been a sensible question to ask, Beulah thought afterwards when it was too late to ask it.

Beulah moved out of the view of the parlour window. Plucking off a whole branch of lilac, she kicked it over the low privet hedge, 'What is lucky?' she asked Hester.

'You're the luckiest woman alive,' said Mrs Treadle, her face zooming into Beulah's out of the darkness. Mrs Treadle's eyes and nose were distorted like Beulah's reflection when she polished the taps in the bathroom. 'If you fell against the tube column, you'd have cracked your head open like a soft-boiled egg.'

'Where am I?' asked Beulah, feeling boards under her back and legs and a soft cushion under her head.

'You're on the floor. I put a pillow under your head. I found

44

you here on the ground unconscious. Now I'm not sure that you haven't given your neck a twist. How does it feel?'

'I was trying to get my ring off,' Beulah tried to sit up and Mrs Treadle pushed her flat again.

'I said *only* if you can manage to take it off, it makes for a better picture.' Mrs Treadle sighed. 'How do you feel?'

'I don't feel lucky anyway,' Beulah rubbed the back of her neck. The buzzer was going incessantly in the waiting room and there was the sound of footsteps. A tall dark man in a dark suit stood over her body. His beard was blue black over a brilliant white shirt, his brown eyes small and glistening like sultanas, his skin like burnt almonds, 'Ah, Mrs Treadle! Is this some new X-ray view that I should be learning about?'

'No, it is not, Dr Kumar. She needs to be examined. Fell down off her chair if you don't mind, while I was out of the department getting chemicals. If you look at her now, I can get on with the rest of them.'

'Who is this?' Dr Kumar asked respectfully. He was trying not to smile at Mrs Treadle, pawing the ground with her shiny shoes, 'Mrs Beulah Kingston, in for X-rays of her hands. Fell off the chair while I was up in theatre.'

'You really should have an assistant,' said Dr Kumar to Mrs Treadle. Kneeling down beside Beulah, he held her wrist between his long brown fingers. A sweet musky cloud drifted over Beulah's face. Dr Kumar was wearing perfume.

45

Chapter Six

The Poleites frowned upon perfume for women, they wouldn't have dreamt of a man wearing it. Dr Kumar's fragrance haunted Beulah for days. She knelt at the old stone trough outside the scullery, rubbing towels in Surf. Fabric conditioners were the nearest Beulah got to perfume; she liked Comfort best but it was good to change them around, the lemon and the spring, the primrose and the pine forest smells. Of the two sisters, Hester was the most concerned with Poleite thrift, so Beulah told her that fabric conditioners extended the life of materials. She didn't believe it for a minute, she just liked the smell of them and the pretty pink, green and white plastic bottles.

'Did I ever think I'd live to see the day!' Hester liked to exclaim when she examined the price of them.

Beulah's neck did seem stiff now and she had to lean back to relieve it every now and then. There was headache, too. It came and went, like someone opening and closing a vice, but she didn't want to believe in it. Dr Kumar and Mrs Treadle had mentioned headache and stiffness and she feared that they had planted the idea of them in her mind.

After her fall, Dr Kumar wrote out another request form for X-rays of her skull and neck but Beulah refused. Once Beulah refused, Dr Kumar stopped looking at her and she almost wished that she had agreed so that he would look at her again. Over her head and with his face away from her, Dr Kumar asked Mrs Treadle to keep the form on one side in case Beulah changed her mind and decided to come back for the X-ray. She knew that he wasn't being deliberately cruel. He had just lost interest.

Mrs Treadle hung the form on a bright yellow clip over her desk, 'You only have to ring me up and I'll fit you straight in.'

'We're concerned for you,' Mrs Treadle insisted, as Beulah filled out the accident form they had produced. But Beulah shrank in fear.

'I can't draw any more of this on top of myself,' she muttered. Dr Kumar and Mrs Treadle exchanged looks.

The Reverend Moylan was never far from Beulah's thoughts these days. His predictions and pronouncements were beginning to sound irrevocably true. In her youth he had been a kind of large and tiresome fly. She had not given him much thought except to avoid him when she could. Now, he was foremost in her mind, his blue eyes bulging. 'They go into hospital with a cold and come out in a wooden box!'

Beulah's thumbs ached, she thought that they were beginning to look distorted. But exercise helped. Joe Costello had told her so and she wanted to believe it. She wished that she had stuck to the old Poleite ways. 'Work those limbs,' said Reverend Moylan. 'Pains are imps that have been sent to try us, give into them and they have you in their thrall.'

Beulah stood up to relieve her aching neck and her knees seemed to give, she wanted to cry but she didn't give in. Apart from needing to remain strong for herself, Hester was likely to come upon her crying and she would have to endure Hester's kind of comfort, a frantic fussing that was no comfort at all.

Standing up, she could see over the wall to where the stream ran through the garden on its way to the whitewashed trough.

47

Hester was the gardener, she spent as long weeding and planting as Beulah spent washing. But even before Hester had moved in, that garden had been beautiful. More beautiful when it was wilder, before Hester came and cut back the straining fuchsia hedge. She remembered the dark night, feeling her way through the high grass and bushes. The way she had sat on the wooden seat under the water-wheel and the long blades of grass came up as far as her shin bones.

The touch of an infidel, the smell of grass and pine that was nothing like the perfume of fabric conditioner. The music coming from Danny Fox's gramophone, crackling under the trees. Forbidden music, they could do nothing about because it came from the other side of the big stone wall.

Poleites were not allowed radios, gramophones or television. Not even hymns. 'Who needs songs when we've got King David singing like a thrush from the pages of the Bible,' Reverend Moylan spat with excitement and his hands trembled on the Bible as he swayed like a black loose-feathered crow.

Judge me, O Lord; for I have walked in mine integrity: I have trusted also in the Lord; therefore I shall not slide. Examine me, O Lord, and prove me; try my reins and my heart . . . Beulah's reins and her heart had been found wanting.

A Poleite was not allowed to look upon his wife's face during the terrible act. It was assumed that a wife wouldn't even want to look and Beulah didn't. Sex was not a modern thing, and certainly not invented by doctors, but Samuel Pole and all Poleites were afraid of it. Maybe it was because it led to childbirth, which could lead to death and Poleite wives were often hard to replace. Or more likely it was because it might become enjoyable, like sugar and cake. It could lead to dangers like music or dancing. Furthermore, Poleites covered up their bodies so much by day, it would be too much of a shock to see each other completely divested by night. Bodies were deadly, they had to be suppressed and covered. 'Poleites have to be propagated, but you musn't look,' Hannah repeated the Reverend Moylan's words to Beulah a week before she got married. 'See no evil,' Hannah said then after a few minutes of puzzled silence from Beulah.

Beulah closed her eyes and breathed in lilac, the water-wheel clanked rhythmically. The trees rushed this way and that, casting curly-headed shadows, cows lowed, a late train went by down at the bottom of the next field. The noise stood out sharp and staccato, the way it always did when there was rain coming.

The next day, Beulah joined in fervently with the Reverend Moylan in the parlour, so fervently that it made him look at her. No one was allowed to outdo the Reverend. The smell of lilac came in the parlour window. 'The Lord's perfume', said the Reverend Moylan.

I am a worm and no man . . . Many bulls have compassed me: strong bulls of Bashan have beset me round. I am poured out like water, and my bones are all out of joint: my heart is like wax; it is melted in the midst of my bowels . . . They part my garments amongst them . . . Deliver my soul from the sword, my darling from the power of the dog.

Beulah had got rid of all the dogs on the farm. Years and years of dogs on Kingston's farm and Beulah silenced them all. Bertie was broken-hearted afterwards, 'Look at the way the cats are multiplying,' he said.

Joe was like King David's Lord, his 'lovingkindness' was before her eyes. Soon he would be qualified, sitting in his father's surgery, taking and giving life. 'With no divine right to do so,' said Reverend Moylan.

When Beulah met Joe down at the Cross, he always stopped to talk. And in front of Danny Fox too. Danny Fox was less dirty

49

then, his hair in an oiled ripple combed back from his forehead. Hanging around the Cross with a Woodbine permanently stuck to his wet lower lip. He cast brazen looks at Beulah, 'Do you notice the evenings are drawing in?' he asked her.

'No, I don't,' said Beulah.

Joe stood next to Beulah and stared Danny down while saying hello and enquiring in his neighbourly way about Danny's mother. The mention of Danny's mother always knocked the leer out of Danny. Beulah wondered if that was why Joe mentioned her even though Joe seemed to be genuinely interested in people's ailments.

'Everything boils down to science,' he told Danny. Beulah stared at the way two fervent lines appeared between Joe's eyebrows when he became serious.

Danny's mother suffered from gout. 'Oh, the high living is right!' went Danny, and then to annoy Joe, 'But you can't beat the home cures though!'

When Danny had walked on, Joe told her different bits of news. Who had been elected. Who was going off to Templemore to train as a guard. How Danny had broken his ankle doing the jitterbug at the Savoy. Yes, that's what the dirty white thing on his foot was. A plaster of Paris cast to set the broken bone.

Plaster of Paris. Penicillin. Surgery. Subconscious . . . Beulah listened to the strange words. It was only two or three minutes at the Cross. His donkey-brown eyes, the shining white parting in his turf-coloured hair, his chocolate-coloured suede gaiters. Beulah tried to hide her big black shoes under her long dress.

Once when Joe came up to her outside the shop, Beulah was carrying a bag with six loaves of bread, the Reverend Moylan having given her special dispensation from baking because Louis was ill. Joe's face was white, 'Glenn Miller is dead. He was killed in a plane crash.'

'Who?'

50

'Glen Miller, the jazz man.'

Beulah had heard that jazz was the devil's music and she knew that Danny Fox played it in the cowhouse where his mother couldn't hear it.

Joe stared at Beulah, 'I've got his records,' he said. She nodded slightly, sensing Danny Fox approach, his voice harsh and cracked between them, 'Have you heard the news, hah? Shot down in the prime of his life, hah?'

Beulah's heart hammered all the way home as she wondered if the plane was shot down or was it a figure of speech. She knew that Danny Fox was fond of figures of speech. 'There was a gale out last night, t'would whip the fingers off you and come back for your hands!'

Sometimes Beulah heard the music rise like a brass cat, coming on a breeze over Danny Fox's stone walls. Dead man's music stretching and crackling from across the farmyard.

Beulah knelt to her sudsy towels once more. Dead men's music always on the farm and a dead dog barking too. A border collie appeared in the yard three years after Louis's death.

It was a hot day, Beulah had given Leah and John a special treat. She put them right into the stone trough with a bar of Sunlight soap and some enamel cups and jugs. They were happy there in the shade of the porch, making bubbles, pouring and emptying from the white and navy-blue enamel vessels.

Beulah was shelling peas, her big feet angrily swollen from the heat and the weight of wool clothes that she had to carry. She jumped when she saw the dog appear across the cobbled yard. How could she have not heard it? At first she thought that it was Rex, Danny Fox's sheepdog. It was also a bit like Ranger, Louis's dog that was poisoned two years before she got married. Han had Danny Fox down for the poisoning, but Louis would never hear a word against Danny Fox then. Even when he was leering at Beulah, Louis said that Danny was just shy.

51

As it came closer she could see that the dog had different markings from Rex and Ranger. Then she saw the tiny white tip to the tail, exactly the same as her own dog Shep who had been put down two years before. The dog approached the stone trough noiselessly, its mouth grinning with thirst, but when Beulah ran up to drive it away, the dog erupted into piercing yelps and her hand went right through its disappearing form.

She could have pretended that it was the heat, her imagination and her uneasy mood that made her see Shep, if only John hadn't started screaming with fear, shaking and shrieking before she had time to get a towel. As she picked up his drenched body, which was plastered with big soft lumps of Sunlight soap, a fragment of soap got into her eye and stung fiercely. She pulled his wet body against her heavy wool dress, as if she could press the images away from his mind completely.

But for days afterwards, John was afraid to go anywhere on his own. He said that he was afraid that the dog with the long mouth would come back.

It seemed to Beulah that the more she remembered the past, the more her thumbs ached. But that was in her mind too. Her thumbs, her neck, her head and a ribbon of pain at the base of her spine.

She stood up again, and as she did she heard Hester calling. 'Beulah, Beulah.' She sounded excited. Beulah tried to jump up quickly, but the pain in her back tugged at her quickly as if she was a dog on a leash. She groaned and staggered, then pulled herself up anyhow and ran to the house.

She saw them standing in the garden, Hester and the tall girl. They both had their backs to her and she could just catch the end of Hester's sentence, '. . . *very* worried about the X-ray. Of course as Dr Costello says . . .'

'Hester!' shouted Beulah in a hoarse voice.

The girl turned around first. She was quaint-looking, familiar

52

too. Her hair was braided into two long plaits that nearly reached her waist and she wore a long dark skirt with a woollen plaid shirt buttoned up to her cream-coloured throat. Beulah stared at the girl and the girl looked back at her, shyly, as if she was expecting something.

Hester had turned around now as well, she caught hold of the girl's hand and brought her forward, 'I had no notion, myself. Who is this big tall girl? I was asking myself.' Hester nodded at Beulah, also looking expectant.

Beulah stared back, 'Are you one of the hippies from Ballinamona?'

Hester gave a nervous laugh, 'For the Lord's sake, Beulah, it's Beccy, your grandchild. Can you not see she is the head off yourself?'

'Beccy,' said Beulah. Her back was on fire.

Beccy took a step forward, Beulah took a step forward. Beccy put out her hand, Beulah shook it solemnly.

'We haven't seen you since you were three,' Hester said. 'Do you remember us at all?'

'I can only remember a man in a long grey coat,' said Beccy, her voice was low and rhythmical, like someone humming under her breath. Beulah didn't want her to stop talking.

'A man,' said Hester, putting her hand up to her girlish brow. 'A man! That's a puzzle now. There hasn't been a man here since, Lord, your daddy passed away.'

'I remember him,' insisted Beccy. 'A big tall man. He had cubes of sugar in his pocket for his donkey and he used to give some of them to me.'

'Oh, Danny Fox!' exclaimed Hester in a relieved voice. 'Do you remember his old donkey. What was she called?'

'Rose was the name of the donkey,' said Beulah, making a sour face. 'What was he doing around you? How did Leah allow you?'

'Leah liked him,' Beccy said, in an injured voice.

53

'Yes, they were pure mad about each other when Leah was young,' Hester agreed. 'Do you remember the two of them playing forty-five on the top of the small stone wall? That was around the time you were teaching John to ride his bicycle, I suppose.'

Beulah looked at Hester, 'We'll go and make the tea,' she said.

She would have liked to have kept holding Beccy's hand. Did Hester mean to hurt her, she wondered, reminding her of John like that. She could never forget those long evenings up and down the lane. The sun and the shadows of lime trees, travelling over and back across John's face.

'Mama, Mama! Don't let go of the saddle, Mama!'

'I'm holding it, I'm holding it.'

'You're not, I can feel it.'

But he always got it wrong. She waited for him to relax and forget about whether her hand was off or on. When she did finally take her hand off, he cycled off down the lane as graceful as a young showjumper. She ran quickly after him, she couldn't wait to tell him when he got to the end that he had been cycling all on his own. Just as he reached the turning for the farmyard, a big shadow fell across him. A tree falling. Beulah screamed and covered her eyes. But when she opened her eyes again, there he was, cycling round and round in circles, 'I'm all right, Mama. What's wrong with you? Have you noticed at all? I'm doing it myself, you don't need to hold the saddle anymore.'

Beulah kept looking up at the trees, she couldn't believe that there wasn't one down.

'Mama, Mama,' John kept saying, until she put her arm around him and told him that he was the best boy in the whole world. Leah passed by, shuffling a pack of cards, ignoring them and John behind her shouting, 'Leah, Leah, I can cycle!' Leah hugged him tight when he was away from Beulah. Leah loved John too. They all did.

54

But after that evening Beulah lived in dread of the trees. They creaked in the wind all the time. She held her breath every time one of the family passed up the drive. She would have asked Danny Fox to have a look at them only she was too proud. And she couldn't say anything to Hester about it because Hester would have called Danny Fox like a shot. Beulah dreamt about the trees falling, her life a secret misery for a whole year. Bad dreams and holding her breath. Drowning in a brown and green forest and she couldn't even talk to Hester. Then John died and she forgot all about it until now.

'Your whole life flashes in front of your eyes!' Louis told her when she was ten and they were playing in the barn. Beulah was supposed to be drowning and she had to call out the key moments in her life while Louis swam through the hay to rescue her. 'Shep learns to give the paw, Rose the Friesian is killed in a flash of lightning, the Reverend Moylan brings us a chocolate cake from Bewleys of Dublin. The Reverend Moylan eats half the chocolate cake himself by mistake.'

Beulah thought maybe she was going to die now, the way she was remembering everything. Except it was not in a flash, it was intermittent, like when she had the car wipers down to the lowest mark and she didn't think they were wiping at all and then they'd strike across the windscreen suddenly. Remembering was a sign of old age.

'Remember in Louis's mother's time when the orchard was a real orchard!' said Hester, clasping her hands. 'Plums and cherries and apples. What I wouldn't give to have the strength to bring it back.'

The table was covered with cups and saucers because Hester wasn't able to count with the excitement of seeing Beccy. Five packets of biscuits were placed on top of five plates. Beulah saw that Hester wasn't able to take the biscuits out of packets and arrange them on the plates, because her hands were shaking too much. Beulah would have helped if she could, except that

55

Beulah's own hands were shaking so much, she had to keep them hidden right under the table. Beccy's face was too rapturous, Beulah thought. Her face lit up as she listened to Hester's account of plums and cherries. She stood up, thoughtfully putting the biscuits out on plates. There were far too many biscuits, they all knew it but they were afraid to say anything that might highlight the shaking of the old women's hands.

'Kimberly, Mikado, Coconut Creams, Lemon Puffs and Kerry Creams, all my favourites,' said Beccy, adding carefully, 'I could give you a hand.'

'A hand with what?' said Hester whose hands, by now, were well hidden under the table. 'The kettle's boiled, Beccy, you might as well fill up the teapot. I've the tea leaves in already.'

'To dig the garden,' said Beccy.

Beulah gave a little frightened jump. Why was Beccy here? How long was Beccy staying? And where was Leah? Had Hester asked Beccy any of these questions? They didn't know anything about Beccy at all, she could be up to anything. She could be on drugs. What had Leah told them over the phone that really counted? Her hair was long and black, well, they could see that, but what comfort was that to anyone? Beccy didn't look like much of a step-dancer either with her awkward ankles showing at the mouth of her brown laced shoes, the fact that she read George Eliot was neither here nor there. Had Leah put Beccy up to getting them to sign the house and land away?

'You can't go digging up the orchard, it's a graveyard now, sure,' Beulah's voice sounded harsh even to herself. 'Louis's dogs are buried there, I will not have you disturbing their bones. And especially Shep, she was the dog that grew up with me. We were born the same week. I brought her with me when I got married.'

Beccy's mouth opened to say something but Beulah swept on, 'Why are you here, anyway, and where is Leah?'

56

Hester pulled her shaking hand out from under the table, her lower lip began to shake as well, Beulah had never seen it do that before. 'Leave the girl alone, she's taking a holiday from Dublin for a while!'

'I've run away from home,' said Beccy.

'How in the name of God could you be running away from home at eighteen years of age?' Beulah was afraid that Beccy's plait was about to fall into the jug of milk, she wanted to reach across and catch it, but Beccy's face and Hester's face with her trembling lip began to whirl round and round and, for the second time that week, Beulah lost consciousness.

Beulah woke in the parlour. At first she thought that she smelt lilac but as she opened her eyes, the sensation went away. Beccy, glowing white, in a man's shirt with no collar, knelt by the side of her sofa, orange and yellow trees swayed outside the window behind Beccy's head. Even though it was late autumn, the warm dry weather had kept the leaves upon the trees. But it was the month of May that was on Beulah's mind. The month of lilac and bluebells.

'You'll have to take it easy, Hester says that you're doing too much washing,' Beccy was like a child playing at being a grown-up.

Hester's fluffy head nodded in the background, 'You'll wear yourself out. Beccy is helping me to take down the B&B sign later.'

All along, Beulah couldn't wait for the B&B sign to come down, now it seemed like a death toll. 'How can I rest with Beccy wanting to dig up the orchard. Has anyone any respect for the ground where poor Shep is buried?'

'I don't want to dig anything, I just want to help,' said Beccy.

'I don't believe that for a minute,' said Beulah, wondering at the words that were coming out of her, after waiting so tenderly for Beccy for years.

'Beulah, what's wrong with you!' exclaimed Hester, and Beulah lapsed into an embarrassed silence. 'She's overworked, that's what wrong,' Hester's head bobbed back and forth as she addressed Beccy. 'And she hates being reminded of Shep, that was her best friend, you know.'

'But Mummy always said that *you* were Beulah's best friend, Hester!'

'Oh no, Shep always came first before me. Wasn't there one night we thought Shep had gone after sheep and I had the measles. Beulah had me round the side of the house, whistling in my nightdress until all hours. I wouldn't mind but measles were a very serious business then, all sorts of people died from them.'

'Did they?' said Beccy.

'Didn't our aunt Susan die of measles? Our mother's sister. If our mother knew what Beulah was up to, she'd have got a good beating with the ash plant.' Hester took a peppermint-coloured linen cushion cover from her sewing basket and began to stab it delicately with an embroidery needle.

Beulah tried to sit up but she fell back, suddenly weak. 'I'm glad to see that you've got over your fit of the shakes, anyway,' she said, looking at Hester's red embroidering fingers.

Hester looked angry for a moment but she composed herself and went on talking as if she was ignoring an embarrassing child. 'Of course I would never tell our mother, but she put me through the mill, I can tell you,' Hester kept going without taking a breath, all as if Beulah wasn't even in the room. 'And it is no wonder that I didn't tell when your Nan was such a great pincher. That was the size of it. I had purple mushrooms up and down my arm from her. And of course they were never seen, we were so well covered up.'

Beulah tossed on the sofa impatiently. 'Will you let me talk for myself, at least!'

But Beccy's shining eyes were directed on Hester. 'And did it affect you?'

58

'What affect me?' Hester stuck out a pink tongue and began to lick her embroidery thread into a point. Beulah thought she looked disgusting.

'Did standing out all night, whistling, bring you to death's door?' asked Beccy.

'Funny thing, the illness turned for the good that night. Imagine though, I could have died.'

'People died from all sorts of simple things then, things they would never die from nowadays . . .' Beccy's voice trailed off. Beulah supposed that Leah had told Beccy all about John. She didn't like to think about what kind of a complexion Leah would have put on the case.

'Poor Johnny,' said Hester, adding, thoughtlessly, 'there was no need for him to die. Not that it was your fault at all,' she turned around to Beulah.

'And who was screaming at me when I was trying to put him in the trap?'

'I was only screaming because it was too late!'

'I thought you wanted to hear about Shep?' said Beulah, ready to talk about anything now except John.

'I still do,' said Beccy.

'I might as well tell you myself. I am the best qualified for it.'

'You are, of course,' said Beccy.

'It was some crowd of infidels behind the whole thing, trying to get Shep blamed for chasing sheep. Sheep were going missing all the time, and these fellows, they were townies, were stealing the sheep themselves. They had the poor creature locked up every night in the old railwayman's cottage. If she hadn't freed herself that night, running home with the rope still attached to her neck, we would never have found out. Poor old Sheppie.'

'She was the same age as Beulah, you know,' Hester said.

'Well, some dog had to be born with the same birthday as me, I suppose. But it wasn't the same year. I was three the day Shep was born. Lord, she was lovely. Soft black and white, the most intelligent dog. She could shake hands, answer the door. She would hang up the Reverend Moylan's cane on the hallstand every Sunday, when he arrived. He was mad about her, brought her sugar lumps once and we nearly fainted.'

'Why did you nearly faint?'

Beulah looked at Beccy. 'Are you pretending or what? Didn't Leah tell you that the Poleites believed greed was the most deadly of sins. The Reverend abhorred sugar especially, although I have to say that *I* think it's the greed for land and property is the root of all evil.'

Beccy didn't flinch. 'I think land and property is a great thing, I would love to have some. It must be great to have something to work hard at, not to be thinking your own thoughts all the time.'

Beulah stared at Beccy, but her face was as innocent and pink as a sunrise. 'Tell me about Shep, did she go everywhere with you?'

'Farmers didn't have time to supervise their children then, that's why some of them ended up at the bottom of wells. I was lucky, Shep was my minder.' Beulah sat back and began to finger her blanket.

'Go on,' said Beccy.

'That's it,' said Beulah, lying and enjoying the thwarted look on Beccy's face. 'I can't remember another single thing about her.'

When Shep died, Beulah was eighteen and Louis twenty. Beulah preferred to think of Shep dying, when in fact, and she couldn't get away from this fact, Shep had been killed and she was to blame. Beulah pleaded with Louis, saying that Shep was never going to recover properly from her accident, that she would be in pain for the rest of her life if she wasn't put down.

60

But the real reason was to stop Shep barking jealously when she went out to the water-wheel.

She got Louis to do it for her. 'Put her out of her misery,' she begged Louis, even though he didn't approve of killing animals. It had the smell of intervention about it. Playing God or doctor.

Yet Louis would do anything that Beulah asked, so he put the gun to Shep's head. Beulah often tried to believe that it was for the best, that Shep was too old. If she had gone to a vet at the time he would have recommended putting her to sleep and that might have been kinder than shooting her. Kinder to Louis too. But Poleites didn't believe in medicine for animals any more than they believed in medicine for humans.

When Beulah was young, she had thought so many of the Poleite laws were written in stone, a very long time ago, but in fact Samuel Pole's horrified reaction to Darwinism was little more than a hundred years ago. Many Victorians had toppled over into Catholicism, but for Samuel Pole it was the start of a great movement. A lot of this information had come to Beulah from Leah, Leah got it from her husband Peter, the historian.

Leah told Beulah that the academic Poleites, all three of them, had come to the conclusion, piecing together old letters, that Samuel Pole's distinctive beard was due to the fact that he was unable to grow hair on the rest of his face but was desperate to cover up the scars on his throat where he had been mauled by an infidel he had been trying to convert. These conclusions were never completely proved and, as Leah wasn't speaking to Beulah after John's death, she never heard any more about it.

Because Samuel Pole's laws were not written down, Poleites, while appearing to be very rigid about their adherence to Samuel's rules, were often inclined to pick and choose. The Rattigans of Churchtown, for instance, refused to have the electricity installed but continued to use gas lighting.

The strong emphasis on the evil of greed among the Poleites

61

of Munster and especially around Two Mile Cross was due to Reverend Moylan and the worry his own sweet tooth caused him. To a Poleite with no access to a dentist, a sweet tooth was a painful and terrifying addiction. The Reverend Moylan preached accordingly.

It was said, now, by the younger Poleites, like Leah, that the Poleite rules had been thought up by Samuel Pole to cover up his own fear of doctors and hospitals. In Samuel Pole's time, hospitals were dangerous. And maybe it was still sensible to stay away from them.

But Leah wasn't a Poleite. All that was left now was the children of Poleites. Hester said that she heard there was a real old-style Poleite man in his twenties living somewhere in Tipperary, but how could he be a proper Poleite without a minister to guide him? The children of Poleites were different and they couldn't understand.

Although Samuel Pole never directly said that sickness was a judgement from God, that's what most of the Poleites believed. And a lot of Catholics besides. In the old days, sickness in the family was a stigma, no matter what foot one kicked with. Sick animals too. Beulah remembered the blessing of the cattle at Fox's. It was hardly noticable that Poleites didn't allow vets on their land because very few people called for the vet or could afford him then.

If Darwin was right and half of her always believed that he was, then she was related to the animal world, which made her a true murderer. Shep always knew what she was thinking. From the very moment the idea of killing Shep had popped into Beulah's head, Shep had huddled against her legs and whined constantly. And Beulah didn't waste any time. It was eleven o'clock in the morning when she decided and Shep was killed before the Angelus bell rang down at the Cross.

Shep's dark eyes rolled all that day and a tremble extended from her nose to the white tip of her bushy tail. Shep knew and

Beulah knew that she knew. 'As sure as there is a harp in a ha'penny,' Danny Fox would have said.

Shep had shared her whole life for fifteen years. But it was a funny thing the way it was always said in the family that they were born on the very same day, when it was only that they celebrated their birthday at the same time of the year. If questioned properly, Bertie would say that Beulah was three the day Shep was born. And that had to be right, for what dog would still be alive, barking and making a nuisance of herself when she was eighteen years of age? Still, Beulah had memories of Shep as a puppy when she herself was six weeks old that she knew couldn't be right but were planted firmly and clearly in her mind. Tangible sharply outlined pictures of Shep, black-nosed and furry-coated, jumping and running among the bales of hay, while Beulah lay swaddled in her little wooden cradle.

The cradle was real, that was for sure. Bertie Kingston had made it for Han Kingston, finishing off the two carved roses at the head while Han was in labour. Bertie said that the calming effect of the woodcarving had helped to get him through. He had had lessons from Louis's great uncle Georgie, who had learned hand-carving when he was going through his William Morris phase, in the days when Louis's family were glamorous and had links with the fashionable world. Great Uncle Georgie never became a Poleite but he grew old on the farm and his hobbies were supposed to be innocent enough, although Bertie heard that he had been on the stage, once, in his youth.

There were special small hand-embroidered sheets which fitted the cradle exactly. Han had made half a dozen pairs, all with different motifs: ivy leaves, buttercups, daisies, tulips, roses, even tiny fir-tree ones for Christmas. Bertie wasn't too sure if they weren't a bit indulgent, but he was very proud of his wife's work.

Six years later, six-year-old Beulah was tucking three- or was it six-year-old Shep into the old rocker, wiping her nose with a

63

fir-tree pillow case, 'Blow, girl, blow your nose,' Shep's head lolling back on the buttercup sheets, her muddy tail hanging out over the bottom of the rocker.

'Like a devil,' said Han, dealing Shep a cruel blow across the side of her head.

They left the rocker in the kitchen for weeks afterwards, with the muddy paw-marked sheets diplayed for everyone to remember Beulah's naughtiness. Eventually, after an age of Beulah begging, they allowed her to scrub the sheets. That's when she developed her taste for washing out of doors, that sunny day, when she was allowed to wash away the paw marks, Shep at her side, patiently allowing Beulah to balance soap bubbles on her pointed black nose.

Chapter Seven

Beulah woke next morning. The sun came in the parlour window, streaming a pattern of bird shapes from the lace curtain across the floor. Sunbeams fell on the Singer sewing machine, showing up the yellow lines in the dark wood. It was half past eight, she had never been in the parlour at this time of the morning and then to be lying down as well, it felt odd. This room had always been the Reverend Moylan's domain. His place to thunder and whisper and lilt.

Who coverest thyself with light as with a garment: who stretchest out the heavens like a curtain.

Beulah lifted her head to sit up, it felt stiff and her neck refused to obey. A violent pain went shooting down her arm, making her cry out. She fell back on the cushions. What had happened? Was she seizing up? She feared that her scream would bring Hester and Beccy running in to sort her out. Bundle her off to the county hospital for that skull and neck X-ray. The word skull made her think of Joe Costello down at the Cross all those years ago talking about Darwin and the scientists examining apes' skulls, looking for the Missing Link.

'I don't care if we are descended from apes,' Joe had said, thrilling her. 'Animals are nicer than people,' he said looking at her with admiration. Beulah was afraid that he was thinking she was a kind of animal. The Lord only knew what queer ideas Catholics

65

had, with their priests and their droning and their incense dispensers. Their relics, and what were their relics? only bits of skulls. Bertie said that those relics were any old bones to fool the people. Not even human, not to mind saints' bones. 'Cows or sheep, anything they can lay their hands on!' No wonder Joe believed Darwin so easily. He did say that all the old-timers were dead against it, but even so, Catholics had to be a gullible crowd.

Beulah waited, holding her breath and pressing her hands against the side of the sofa. Already, little flames of pain began to lick the base of her thumbs. *Lord, Lord, Lord*, she began to intone under her breath.

Minutes went by, then an hour and still no one came. Surely Hester at least, would come, Beulah hoped desperately. She didn't know what time it was. Where could Hester be? She hoped that Beccy wasn't a smoker. What if she was smoking in the bedroom? Could she be having a morning cigarette? Once, they had a man staying as a guest and he had three cigarettes before he came down for breakfast. It was the using of the soap dish as an ashtray that really upset Beulah. Every bedroom in the house had its matching Victorian set and they were used properly.

Apparently, they were a fashion item now, a guest had told Beulah once. 'Is it fashionable to wash with cold water too?' Beulah had asked and the guest, a flower-arranging big farmer's wife had answered, 'God no, you wouldn't want to break them, they're antiques,' and gave Beulah a funny look.

Beulah still used her dark blue ewer, rising early to fill it in the stream. She stood in her liberty bodice to wash in icy clean water. She wondered what would happen that comfort now? Pain suddenly shot down her left arm. At half past ten, for the first time in her life, Beulah called for Hester.

Hester poked her white-haired head around the door.

'I thought that you'd all gone!' Beulah tried to twist her stiff neck in Hester's direction.

66

'I was going quietly so as not to disturb you, I thought you'd need a long sleep after your faint and the X-rays and all.'

'I suppose Beccy is still in bed, I hope she doesn't smoke. What's the point in putting lavender in the sheets, then!' Beulah was gasping with pain.

Hester ran to the couch, 'Beccy was up late worrying about you and she's not the only one. What's wrong, you're all bent. Have you a crick in your neck or what?'

Tears rolled down Beulah's cheeks like hot tar, 'Hester, I can't move.'

At twelve o clock, Beccy was clumping up and down the hall in her strong laced shoes, waiting for the ambulance.

'I don't need an ambulance!'

'Well, you can't get into the car the way you are, try and relax, they said it might be a while.' Beccy had the face of a saint, her plaits were very long, although not as long as Beulah's hair had been when she was a young girl. To try and take her mind off her own pain, more than anything else, Beulah asked Beccy, 'Why are you here, anyway?'

She did not expect Beccy to reply: 'It is to do with religion.'

'But, sure there's no Poleites left here or anywhere!' Beulah exclaimed in amazement.

'There is that young Poleite living in Tipperary,' Hester said, sounding pleased. 'I think we should contact him.'

Beccy shook her head and continued to clump up and down the hall, she clasped her hands in front of her. 'No, don't! I mean I don't mind but what I'm really worried about is Mummy.'

Hester and Beulah stared at Beccy. Beccy wrapped her right plait around her wrist.

'I know that you must think that I am completely mad!'

'Not at all,' said Hester, her lower lip beginning to shake again.

67

'Completely mad,' said Beulah, her stiff neck felt it had been turned to stone. 'Or very stupid to think you can persuade us that you're worried about your mother when you're after running away from home?'

'She wouldn't want me to marry a Poleite, that's what I mean. She's always saying that I should be glad I'm not being brought up a freak.'

Beulah and Hester exchanged looks.

'I don't think she'd be that worried about me running away really, she's got loads of friends.'

'Of course she'd be worried,' said Hester.

'All her friends ever do is tell her how fantastic she is.'

'Well aren't they nice friends,' Hester said, but before Beccy had the time to answer, Beulah moved her stony lips, 'Stop, stop fooling with your hair, it is very annoying, apart from being the height of bad manners.'

Beulah wished the ambulance would come. 'Young people today are allowed to talk far too much.' Her voice echoed as if it was coming from a stone corridor.

'I was a kind of a Catholic to be honest. I picked it up at school. Leah was always doing things with her friends, they're all into herbalism and homeopathy, astrology and yoga. I just wanted big strong laws to support me, and this priest was helping me, although I wish he had been more definite about some things because he didn't completely agree with the Pope.'

'Who could?' asked Beulah to the ceiling. She was surely turned to stone. All she could move were her eyes.

'And then he went funny?'

'Who?'

'This priest. He said I was asking too many questions. He told me it was the way to Hell. Yet, he told me, on his oath, the first day I met him, that there was no such place as Hell, and I was disappointed then, you know.' Beccy's hands kept reaching for her hair and she kept stopping them just in time. 'Then I

68

thought there's no point in this, my roots are Poleite. Poleites didn't pretend there wasn't a Hell. And I want to believe in Hell, it is much tidier than psychology. I get lost in psychology. It's Hell not having a Hell, you know,' Beccy gave an awkward laugh at her own joke. Hester and Beulah stared at her.

She finished up quickly, 'Leah wanted me to go to university and I didn't want to go because I thought it was a selfish thing to be sitting around for three years reading books when I could be helping people and Leah said that I was selfish not doing what she wanted.'

How did things keep getting worse? Beulah wondered. How were they going to put up with this yearning saint around the house? It was probably Leah who had thrown Beccy out.

Beulah's body had always been strong, never let her down. Her mind had been set, too. She had not agonised about her feelings towards Louis, had gone out to the water-wheel when she knew it was wrong, that was certain, but she had not struggled with her conscience. Not in the least. Scrubbed the house harder, that was all. *Cleanliness is next to godliness*. Her body hadn't given her a scrap of trouble, it was her children who had been the ones with the delicate bodies. Then, without scarcely a warning, just those twinges in her thumbs (if she had her way again, she would put up with them, not go near a hospital) and now she was lying here, like a pillar of stone. Or salt, maybe. Like Lot's wife from too much looking back.

They couldn't help Beccy. The Poleite movement was dead, there were no more ministers to call on. Beulah liked to think that if Reverend Moylan was alive he could come and say, 'Arise, take up your bed and walk!' and she would. But that was a blasphemous thought in itself. Poleites didn't even believe in saints or miracles. Outside of the Bible, miracles, like illnesses, like cures, like saints, were all in the mind. The ambulance men were kind, but Beulah couldn't bear them with their 'One, two, three, lift! Are you all right Missus?' She ignored them. Beccy fussed around them, saying, 'Gently, gently.'

Hester was quiet. She was very worried, Beulah knew. She couldn't let on of course and that cheered Beulah up a bit.

They strapped Beulah's neck into a huge white plastic collar. It felt ugly. Beulah worried that it was not clean. She tried not to think about who might have been last wearing it. Hester stood beside the stretcher while the ambulance lowered a mechanical ramp. The beeping noise was worse than any screech owl.

'I want a proper Poleite funeral,' she hissed at Hester. Beccy made a concerned face.

'You are a big ears,' Beulah said to Beccy.

Beulah said nothing more, her strapped red-blanketed body slid into the ambulance like a corpse going into the flames of a crematorium. She thought of Danny Fox's mother.

When Maggie Fox had her stroke, she cursed Danny from a height. They took her away in the pony and trap, Danny following on his grey mare, the tears streaming down his face. It was the late forties, maybe early fifties. 'It is so, for your own good, Mama,' he kept crying out, and Beulah would not have believed such tenderness if she had not witnessed it there, standing in Fox's boreen with Hester. The mare must have been sixteen hands high, snorting and steaming in the early morning mist. Hester and Beulah had gone down to lend a hand and be neighbourly, but they hadn't been prepared to see Danny like this. Danny, the smart alec, with his hands trembling, tying handknitted slippers on Maggie's purple swollen feet, a litany of mother names flowing from his lips, 'Mama, mammy, mamie.'

And the abuse he got, 'You knitted those slippers too small!'

'Her mind is gone,' Danny told them and took his handkerchief out. 'To see her beautiful face twisted!'

Reverend Moylan stood at the bottom of the lane when the

small procession passed. Dwarfed in the mist, next to the steaming mare, Reverend Moylan swept off his wide-brimmed hat. His head was smooth and small, 'Why won't the doctor allow her die at home?' he roared rhetorically at Beulah.

Afterwards, Reverend Moylan led the way straight to the parlour and read psalm after psalm for Maggie Fox. 'And don't forget her faithful son Michael who misguidedly delivered her into the hands of her enemies. To die in a cold building far from her homestead, her chickens and all her possessions.'

When Maggie Fox died alone in hospital, Danny echoed these sentiments in his own words for nights after her death. Filled with remorse, swaying and staggering around the lanes as if he didn't know where his home was.

'The creature doesn't know where he lives,' Hester said, the night he tried to climb up the drainpipe outside Beulah's window.

Danny shouted, 'Come out, Beulah, and put your arms around me!'

That was the end of Beulah listening to Hester's excuses; she wrenched open the window, shouted 'infidel' and soaked him with a jugful of cold water. Danny didn't have any trouble finding his way home after that. He continued to drink. From time to time he turned up drunk outside Kingston's, usually around the anniversary of his mother's death. But he didn't address Beulah on these occasions, he sang rebel songs like 'James Connolly' and 'Sean South of Garryowen'.

'As if we cared one way or another,' snorted Beulah, who hadn't the slightest interest in either politics or history.

Hours in casualty, then a happy nurse came, smelling of coffee and Marietta biscuits, took her temperature and blood pressure. The hardest part was hearing the nurses chatter and laugh and get on with their conversations. It wasn't that she ever wanted to be pitied, she just couldn't bear to hear them

71

enjoying themselves. She wouldn't have minded being dead, it was her powerlessness that was so unbearable. Less than a week ago, she had worried about not being able to do her washing, now she couldn't even sit up.

Dr Kumar was in theatre, the nurse told her. As soon as he was finished, he would come down to her, the nurse said, adding in an impressed voice, 'He remembers you and all. Didn't you have a fall in X-ray last week with Mrs Treadle?'

Beulah remembered Reverend Moylan's reaction to the news that Sam Potts had had a chest X-ray. 'There is no doubt he was seduced by that woman in the tea shop calling him love.' The Reverend's voice thickened and warbled over the word love, disconcerting his audience in the parlour. They hung their heads while the Reverend collected himself.

'It drove a chink into his brain. Undoubtedly! But to expose the Lord's creation to that devilish machine, his tender rib-bones, his sweet mysterious lungs thrown open like that for all to see what the Lord . . .' and the Reverend Moylan fainted away like a woman onto the parlour floor.

Afterwards, it turned out that the Reverend had tried to give up sugar completely. He was suffering from lack of energy, not from shock, when he fell into what Danny Fox would have called a 'strong weakness'. Disturbed by his ravening sweet tooth, he had abruptly, and without giving proper notice to his body, given up all sugar in his tea, given up cakes, biscuits, jam. Even honey, which he himself had called God's sugar, he gave up suddenly. Han Kingston reminded him of this as she knelt beside his prostrate body with a honeycomb and a spoon. 'You said yourself it was sent from the Lord.' Lying down, the Reverend Moylan seemed a different person, more of a baby really, sticking out his pale tongue to lick the golden honey from Han's best silver spoon.

What was not baby-like, however, was the dark guilty en-joyment in his eyes as he waited for more.

72

To his small community's relief, the Reverend bounded to his feet after four spoons of honey. Han Kingston's diagnosis had been correct, he'd been sugar-starved. Roentgen,' he bellowed, 'was an unfortunate and misguided man. All of them, the whole lot of them, they thought they were helping mankind and they all died roaring. Madame Curie's hands were covered in cancer, and the first technicians, the Lord protect their poor souls, stuck their hands straight into the X-ray beam, to measure the strength of it. The tumours were dripping off them. Oh deadly X-ray! Invisible fire!'

'I suppose I'd better have a few more spoons of honey,' he said to Han Kingston afterwards. 'Have to think of my brethren now. I must not deprive them of their shepherd.'

'X-ray time!' called the coffee-drinking nurse as if she was inviting Beulah to a tea party. 'Dr Kumar can't get down from theatre, but it doesn't matter because he says that he wrote out a form for you last week. He wants your head and cervical spine X-rayed.'

To her dismay, Beulah realised that despite all her fear of the X-rays, she'd been looking forward to seeing and smelling Dr Kumar as a kind of consolation prize. She stared listlessly at the nurse's white plastic badge. Student Nurse Bolton.

'Cervical spine is only another name for your neck,' said Nurse Bolton, kindly.

Beulah was annoyed with Hester for staying in the waiting room like a timid lamb. Other patients' relations insisted on staying next to their loved-ones' trolleys. They had to be chased away like dogs every time the nurse came around and, like faithful dogs, they always came back the minute the nurse had gone off.

Nurse Bolton joined up with a porter and the trolley whizzed away from casualty down long corridors towards X-ray.

Mrs Treadle's face was pale in the gloom, she was helping a

bow-legged man off the table. 'I'm going for the both knee replacements,' he said proudly to Beulah, as she waited with Nurse Bolton while Mrs Treadle got the table ready for her X-ray. Beulah turned her head away from him. The thought of people putting plastic inside their bodies sickened her. Nurse Bolton got into an energetic conversation with the bow-legged man about different types of prosthesis and replacements, about people formerly confined to wheelchairs leaping over nine-bar gates and milking eighty cows and going on holidays to Mexico, only two months after their operations.

'It's marvellous, really.'

'T'is a miracle,' said the man.

As Beulah closed her eyes and thought of Reverend Moylan, there was the squeak of trainers across the shiny polished floor. Sheila Sheehan, 'Beccy told me you were here, hasn't she turned out a fine girl? And I came straight over. Wasn't it fierce lucky I'd the day off? Now, Beulah, you are not to be letting this little setback get you down. It's never as bad as you think. It could be psychological and Beccy thinks you're depressed. Find out what's bothering you and all this could disappear, like that,' Sheila clicked her fingers to include the bow-legged man, Nurse Bolton and Mrs Treadle.

'I wish *you* would disappear,' said Beulah, rudely, reminding herself of Maggie Fox again. Closing her eyes, she lay trembling with fear and humiliation as Sheila questioned the little man upside down and inside out. Was he sure that he was never a jockey?

74

PART TWO

Chapter Eight

The black pump stood like a long face in the middle of the village, and if Bertie Kingston hadn't believed in running water then Beulah would have had an excuse to go to the pump, and there she was bound to meet Joe, whose large new house, complete with balcony and short tree-lined drive, was just a stone's throw away.

For a long time after Beulah had lain on the Costellos' drawing room floor, she thought longingly of the iron pump. How she could stroll down there for a bucket or two and meet Joe again. Renew their friendship over the clear water that was as cold as the stethoscope against her skin.

'I believe in taps and that is that!' said Bertie. 'God knows what germs one would pick up at that old pump with every dog of the road licking it from all angles. It's no wonder the Pyms of Garryowen are so sickly!' Bertie twisted his taps on and off, splashing the front of his flannel shirt.

Poleites liked to talk about other Poleites. The ones that were too fast and the ones that were too antiquated. Stories circulated about remote Poleites, like the Hollands of Skibbereen who wouldn't even wear shop-bought shoes and went around with stinking, badly cured cow-hide sacks tied onto their ankles. 'I don't know if there's any truth in that,' said Han Kingston a hundred times, but Bertie wouldn't be denied his story. Years

77

later, Beulah found out that the Hollands weren't Poleites at all, just Catholics who were a bit touched, couldn't be bothered with shoes and slopped around in dirty torn galoshes.

However, by the time Beulah reached sixteen, the last place she wanted to be seen was at the pump, struggling with buckets of water. One January there was a problem with the water, a pipe burst in the frost. Bertie called Louis over and as they stood in the yard looking and talking under their wide-brimmed hats, Han began to fret, 'How long are they going to stand there? You'll have to go down to the pump, Beulah. Take the new bucket and fill it up.'

Beulah looked at the bucket, horrified. Joe Costello was home on holidays from university. He was a man now, with soft tan gloves and shirts with cuff links. She couldn't bear Joe to see her heaving buckets around like a common servant girl.

Hester looked up from the sheets she was hemming and said, 'I'll go.' Hester was hoping to see Margaret Costello, home from Dublin. Margaret was a year into her domestic science course at Sion Hill College and might be found traipsing around the village in her finery. Hester was always looking for ideas for sewing and making things, she'd copy ideas from anyone. She wasn't worried about heaving buckets in front of anyone, because she thought that there was no higher honour than to be a hard-working Poleite. 'Go on, then,' Beulah said, thrusting the shiny new bucket at Hester.

'Stop right there,' said Han, looking very severe. 'Is it the way Beulah is getting too grand for God's work?'

'Beulah has a bit of a cold.' But Hester was never very convincing.

'You're the one with the cold,' said Han. 'Out that door, Beulah!'

Beulah wore her new black coat, it was long and it was wide, but not half long or wide enough. She would have liked to disappear into it entirely, become a tree or a bush or a bit of a fence so that no one could see her. She shuffled along, kicking the frozen ruts with the toe of her boot. The sight of Louis reminded her that her marriage was only six months away. She gave Bertie and Louis a wide berth, but they still looked up when she passed at the furthest end of the yard. They put their hands up to the brims of their hats to shade against the dazzle of the sun on the frost. Beulah put her hand up too, to give a noncommittal wave but really to block out the sight of them.

When Beulah arrived at the pump, she faced Costello's new house and kept her eyes on the front door. If she saw Joe she was determined to make a run for it, no matter what the outcome.

Holding her coat away with one hand, she began to crank the pump handle up and down. It was humiliating beyond all. She didn't know what she looked like, but it had to be the opposite of Margaret Costello, who had been around the village all Christmas in a scarlet coat with lipstick to match, smelling of roses, collecting holly and visiting the church, when Beulah knew well she wasn't the slightest bit religious. But then they were all like that, the people who went to Mass, bursting out of hats and suits. What kind of a God were they trying to impress? The bucket was nearly full and she hadn't seen a soul. She would be gone soon and no one would be the wiser. 'Thank the Lord,' said Beulah, who hadn't thought about him at all until now.

'Happy New Year to yourself, Beulah,' said Joe Costello, coming up behind her, with a bottle-shaped parcel wrapped in brown paper.

'Oh, Happy New Year,' said Beulah, standing in front of the bucket. She never thought that he might come from the other direction.

'Nellie Sheehan said there is a burst pipe on your farm.'

'Did she?' Beulah kept standing in front of the bucket, glad that her coat was big enough to hide the shakes in her legs.

79

'Do you want a hand with that?' Joe pointed behind Beulah's legs. She felt weak. Was she translucent? She was afraid to talk in her country accent.

Joe picked up the bucket, 'In Jervis Street Hospital, it's the nurses from the country are the best ones, you know.' It felt like he might be giving her an admiring look, Beulah looked ahead stiffly. She did not know how to react to talk about nurses, who were considered minor demons in the Poleite world. Was he comparing her to a nurse? Did she want to be? She did. Anything that he admired.

'Do you get many of them up at the university?' she asked, as her feet snapped the thin ice on the puddles that lined the side of the road.

'Not at the university, in the hospital, I'm there nearly all the time now, because I'm in my final year.'

Beulah felt incredibly trusted yet she couldn't speak. She tried to breathe in a sympathetic way, white tornados of breath steamed into the air in front of her. Joe put the brown bottle-shaped parcel into his pocket and his hand swung as he balanced the bucket. He brushed against Beulah's dress and spots of water fell dark against his tweed trousers.

'I admire women who work hard and are natural. Don't wear makeup.' Joe turned his head around to Beulah. She kept looking straight ahead. 'I think red lipstick is an abomination, unnatural, like the bright arterial blood from a consumptive.'

'What kind of blood?' asked Beulah.

'Arterial, it's bright red because it is oxygenated.'

'You learn beautiful words at the university, *arterial* and *oxygenated*,' Beulah tried the words out herself in a sudden burst of confidence. The syllables rolled around her mouth like acid drops, sweet and sour.

As they came to the top of Kingston's avenue, Joe put down the bucket. 'There's a lot of Latin there all right,' said Joe proudly. 'You don't have much of that do you?'

80

'We have King James's English.'

'Which one now was he? Was he related to Bonny Prince Charlie?' Joe laughed.

Beulah didn't know what to do with herself. She pretended to be dazzled by the sun, put her hand up to her forehead and the wide black sleeve of her coat fell back. Joe reached out and caught her wrist with his right hand, 'That's your styloid process.' He touched the bony knob on the outside of her wrist. 'The styloid process is that projection at the end of your ulna. The radius and ulna are the two bones in your forearm and they cross over about halfway up,' Joe slid his hand halfway up Beulah's arm for a moment and then took it away. He looked embarrassed.

Beulah said, 'It is very interesting.'

'Do you find it interesting? I hope it isn't against your religion.'

'It is not.' Beulah looked away while she lied.

'Well, you know that other little bony projection on your ankle?'

Beulah nodded eagerly, wondering if she should take her boots off.

'That's called the lateral malleolus,' Joe didn't touch her again. 'I better go or they'll be looking for me.' He took the bottle out his pocket. As Beulah's eyes fell upon it, he said, 'Whiskey for father, I don't touch it at all myself.' But he didn't look at her when he said this.

There was the buzz of voices around the turn of the avenue and Beulah quickly picked up the bucket as Louis and Bertie came into view.

'Goodbye, so,' said Joe.

'Goodbye,' said Beulah, not looking at him.

She was still listening to his feet crunching away on the crisp earth when Bertie asked, 'What was that young Costello doing? Was he trying to talk to you?'

81

'He offered to carry the water.'

'I hope you told him, no.'

'I did indeed,' said Beulah tossing her head and trying not to look excited when Bertie said, 'The impertinent pup! He'd get you on your own for one minute and the next thing he'd be trying to take your temperature.'

When Bertie was gone, Beulah touched the bony knob on her wrist. *Styloid process*, she said the words over and over again that night when she was going to sleep. She imagined Joe taking her temperature.

As long as Bertie watched over Beulah, she had no excuse to be hanging around the Cross, collecting buckets of water from the village or anything else besides. The only place she was allowed to hang around was Louis Kingston's farm. Louis Kingston had become ugly and religious. And she was going to have to marry him, as soon as Bertie had persuaded him to install running water.

'Haven't I the water running in the back door?' said Louis jerking his thumb over his shoulder, pulling up his belt, when Bertie had called around with Beulah one Sunday evening the very next summer.

'Son,' said Bertie Kingston. He had called Louis 'son' ever since Louis's father's death four years before. 'Son, you've got to examine the dangers. Germs and babies don't go together. You will have a family soon enough.'

As they walked home through the fields, Beulah wanted to ask Bertie about this family that was going to come to Louis soon enough. She had heard there were Poleite Kingstons in Cashel and were these the ones that were coming to stay with Louis?

But she got no chance to broach this subject with Bertie. They had no sooner turned out of the cobbled yard when Bertie flung his arms up against the red orange sky and exclaimed, 'By

82

Jove! What a boy! No! Take that back! I mean to say, what a man!'

'Louis is it?' asked Beulah, incredulously, relieved to be rid of the sight of Louis and his fluffy juvenile Poleite beard.

'Who else?' asked Bertie, raising his arms to the sunset again. 'Orphaned at fourteen, he did not fall down on the job. He made a great hand of that farm. He could have ran around, oh he could. I couldn't be watching over him all the time with you two maidens to be minding as well. He could have turned into a berserker, oh yes. I heard Danny Fox was offering him drink, but he did not take it. He is a Poleite to be proud of and there will be no prouder man than myself when the two of ye get married.'

Beulah had never expected to be consulted about whom she was going to marry, and she could have guessed that they would want her to marry Louis, but it was still a terrible shock. Bertie was going to lay down the law, whatever Beulah thought. And he was uneasy about it, too. Beulah could see by the way he waved frantically at the dying sun.

'I don't want to be looking after the Kingstons of Cashel,' she burst out in a choked voice.

'What Kingstons of Cashel? It will be just yourself and Louis. God knows, I'm not an ogre. It is not as if I'm selling you off, or anything like it. Poleite boys are hard to come by.' Bertie put his hand on Beulah's shoulder. 'Anyway, ye were always friends weren't ye?'

Beulah didn't answer, she sank into a silence, listening to the crows tearing the air, the ticking of grasshoppers, she thought that she could even hear the dew spilling against her father's long dark clothes as they swept the grass.

It was true that, when they were younger, Louis and Beulah had been the best of friends. When she was younger she had wanted to live with Louis on Hollywood farm. She loved every

83

bit of it. The wide lime-tree-lined avenue swept up to the cobbled yard at the side of the house then divided into two separate paths, one leading to the front of the house with its garden of tiny hedges and the overgrown apple orchard beyond. The other path led to the back garden where the stream ran through into a stone trough just outside the scullery. The stream ran on for about fifty yards and then joined a small river where the water-wheel stood. The wheel was built in 1825, its wooden slats blackened from moisture. The noise of the water was deafening and hypnotic, Beulah could stand there for hours, watching the clanking wheel and the drips of water hanging like clear fingernails from the edges of the wood. The stream flowed on past the mill and then went underground, emerging on the other side of the big ditch that bounded Stanley's field. To the right of the millwheel was the stone wall that divided Kingston's and Fox's farm. A small iron gate connected with Fox's boreen.

Louis had never been handsome, but before he became a teenager, he had a fresh look. Very white skin, fairish brown hair, medium-blue eyes. He wore shorts that came to his knees and his knees were always covered with red marks because he was forever kneeling hard in some place. In the parlour, during service, or beside the trough washing eggs, or on the cobbles in the yard, showing her how to draw letters on an old slate. He wouldn't ever let her be mean to Hester. Later she was often glad about that. After a day on Louis's farm she could kneel down by her bed and not have to say sorry to the Lord for teasing Hester, or pinching her. Or running away from her the time the cows got into the river and Hester was stuck on the opposite bank, crying like a fool.

Beulah knew that she was sometimes unfair to Hester. Maybe it was because she always had Shep, she felt she could do without Hester whenever she felt like it. The temptation was so great. Hester's tearful dependence made Beulah want to walk away and she did so, many times. 'Come on, Shep,' she'd click her tongue, ignoring Hester's woebegone face.

When Hester cried out, 'I hate Shep!' she held out even longer.

'Now I will not talk to you after you insulting Shep!'

The day of the cows in the river, they were down on Kingston's farm. Beulah and Hester, nine and seven, Louis just eleven. The stream had always been an attraction for Beulah and Hester. They never had anything so pretty in their dour black-clothed lives. Louis had some wooden ducks attached to corks and they were floating them. Hester, of course, wanted to keep doing this, over and over, all afternoon. She didn't want to follow it down through the garden and beyond.

'Stay here, then,' said Beulah, meanly, knowing Hester was too terrified to stay behind with Old Louis Kingston. Louis's father was old and rheumy-eyed, his breathing as rough as the stubble on Bertie's cheeks at morning milking time. 'Mr Kingston will mind you. Come on Shep!' She clicked her tongue at Shep impatiently, eager to be off with Louis, but when she turned around Louis was kneeling down next to Hester.

'You think the stream stays clear? It does not, then. It starts going brown at the end of the first field and by the time it gets to Stanley's field it is a big river, the Salley Martin, and there's big long green things growing underneath and I think they're seaweed but I'm not sure, and I often wish that my grand-uncle Georgie was still alive, he knew all those things. They say he was a very educated man.' Louis's smooth head nodded over Hester's small fluffy one. Louis had a knack of not letting Beulah feel left out either, turning around with his old-man's gestures. 'Beulah, wait till we get past Stanley's field, though, and we're down by the railway. There's these lovely kind of white jars that the railway men left behind. I don't know what

85

they are, but they feel silky. Then we've got to cross the railway. (I'll mind you, Hester.) And then we'll be there down where the soldiers used to come out from the barracks, bathing.'

'They won't come out when we're there?' asked Hester anxiously.

'Of course they won't,' said Beulah. 'They're all gone back to England. They're probably even dead by now, shot down from their bombers.'

'Lord have mercy on their souls,' said Louis. 'It is all Kingston land, now.'

'Are you ready now,' said Beulah, taking Hester's hand and they all set off.

But then Hester got too smart. What possessed her in front of Louis Kingston? Down at the shallow end of the soldier's swimming pool, they took off their shoes and socks and paddled. 'I wonder what it is like to be able to swim,' said Louis. 'Do you think it is like flying?'

'I *am* swimming,' said Hester and held her dress up away too high above her knees, plunging around like an ostrich, heading for the other side of the bank, the deepest part of the shallow part of the river.

Beulah wanted to close her eyes at the sight of Hester's legs. Had she no consideration for anyone else's feelings? But Hester had entered her own space, she was too far away for Beulah to pinch her. She bent her knees down low and walked around with the water up to her neck, pretending that she could swim. She went up and down and around the water hole for about five minutes before she turned into one of those berserkers that Bertie always talked about. She went into a kind of screeching fit, roaring out snatches of psalms and twirling herself round, shaking droplets from her dress.

'She's never speaking in tongues, is she?' Louis asked.

Shep followed Hester, deserting Beulah for once, and began

86

to jump around inside the water. 'Can't you hear it?' said Beulah. 'It is King James's English. She's trying to imitate the Reverend Moylan.'

Beulah's hands were over her face. She couldn't bear Louis to think that she had a mad sister and a mad dog, but he only laughed. 'I'm glad anyway she's not speaking in tongues,' he said. 'I'd hate that.'

Beulah took her hands down from her face and looked at him. Why was he so easygoing and why was he not tortured like she was? Growing up a Poleite. Did he not feel ashamed of his queer clothes? Now that he was eleven, Louis wore long black trousers and a long black coat, he acted as natural as anything. At least until he felt Beulah's eye boring into him. Then Louis went red, flicked at his round hairstyle, 'Have I dirt on my face or what?'

That was how the two of them were distracted and they didn't realise that the whole herd of Louis's father's Friesians were heading straight for the river until they were practically on top of them and they had to step back while Hester fled screaming with fear to the other bank. Dragging Shep with her.

'That'll soften her cough,' said Beulah, privately thinking Shep was getting her true deserts as well. Did Shep not know whose dog she was?

Beulah dug her heels into the marshy ground. 'Will we go back to Stanley's field now? I want to pick buttercups for my mother.' It was usually Hester who picked the wild flowers and brought them home. But now, Beulah was thinking, it was Hester who was the bad one. Screeching psalms and getting drenched. Shep the old traitor could rescue her.

'No,' said Louis, and she knew she was beaten straight away, before he'd even waded across. Before he'd come back with Hester on his back and Shep swimming, looking as brave as a dog could.

87

'I've no sympathy for you,' said Beulah, when Shep tried to nose back against her skirt. Then Louis and Hester had to run round and round in circles until they got dry. It took a very long time and Beulah enjoyed that part, calling out, 'Faster and faster!' Louis was enjoying it, too, his face crimson with exertion. But not Hester, she was scared now of getting into trouble. Not that Old Louis would have noticed their wet clothes. He was almost blind. But Han Kingston wasn't when she came in the pony and trap to collect them. She wasn't sure about letting them play with Louis, so she always examined them anxiously when they came back. Bertie had no worries, 'I'd trust that boy with anything, even my two little maidens.'

Beulah had agreed with her father that Louis was special then. He made being good easy for her, the same way he had made reading easy for her when she was little. He'd shown her birds' nests, puppies born in warm tunnels in the hay barn. The same hay barn where he had hidden his grand-uncle Georgie's copy of *The Arabian Nights' Entertainments*. Down in the barn Louis, Beulah and Hester pretended to be Arabians whirling imaginary scimitars through the sunbeams and hay dust. Louis shouting out, *'Alf Layla wa Layla!'* That was the Arabian for One Thousand and One Nights. It said so in the book.

For years, Beulah wished that Louis was her brother. She wished that creepy Old Louis Kingston was dead and they were all living in Louis's farmhouse by the stream. Bertie deserved to have that farm more than Old Louis. He was always saying what a hand he would make of it and what a crying shame it was the way Old Louis was letting generations of farming go to waste.

If only Louis was her brother, Beulah thought, then they could all live in the farmhouse. Hester, Louis and herself sleeping in the same room on couches like Arabians.

But then Louis grew up, began wearing the Poleite hat, and

88

the only thing Arabian about Louis now was his evil genie beard. And it wasn't just the beard and hat that had made Louis so repulsive; Bertie and the Reverend had hats and beards, and though Beulah might have thought that they were stupid-looking, she never found them disgusting. The problem began with Louis when she couldn't think of him as her brother anymore.

It was earlier in the summer that Beulah had come up to the farm with Bertie, 'Where's your father? I'm looking for one of my implements and I think he's got it,' said Bertie, pushing past Louis, running in the door like a jealous bull. Bertie wanted to be generous and he loaned things easily. But the minute his implements left the farm, he wanted them back again. 'I don't mind what they take,' he groaned like a man with colic. 'I'm not accusing them of dishonesty, if I could only trust them not to forget TO GIVE THEM BACK!'

Beulah and Louis were left alone in the yard, Beulah screwing up her face against the evening sun, scrutinising Louis's reddish beard. Louis's face was flushed as Bertie pushed past him. Beulah felt embarrassed, too, because she knew that Old Louis only had the pitchfork for three hours. She was going to say something about it when Louis put his hand up to shield his face. The sun wasn't even in his eyes. The cuff of his black jacket fell away from his wrist, it was all red. Beulah looked at the other wrist. It, too, was all red, as if he had been scraping his styloid processes together. She looked at his neck. Scarlet. His face. Magenta. Louis couldn't look her in the eye, the way she couldn't look Joe Costello in the eye.

Finally Louis managed to say, 'The evenings are drawing in.' Talking like an old man with a pipe except he couldn't have a pipe because he was a Poleite.

Beulah had a feeling that she was going to have to marry him. Some way her father looked at them when he came out of the house brandishing his pitchfork. There wasn't a thing she could

89

have done about it even if she had been sure about what was on Bertie's mind. She was helpless.

They drifted into her sight for a moment but they soon drifted out again, Sheila Sheehan, Nurse Bolton and the man with the jockey legs talking about cured cripples jumping on top of tractors and attending All Ireland Football Finals and training greyhounds.

Beccy did look like her, she had the height and the black hair. But Beccy seemed to be truthful, a good person. A really good person like Louis. Already, Hester was talking about contacting the last Poleite living in Tipperary. That was bound to bring more trouble. She was going to put a stop to those plans once she got out of the hospital. For a moment, Beulah wondered what the last Poleite looked like. But all she could see in her mind was Louis, as he was in 1945. A slight man with a pale face and rosy cheeks, lost in black clothes.

Chapter Nine

Since the day that Bertie went back to claim his pitchfork, Beulah had been acting sour, taking her feelings out on Hester. And craving for sugar. The two sisters were in the pantry every minute that Han's back was turned. Hester with her head stuck in the sour vinegar pickle jars, Beulah going for the bags of sugar. Beulah had to lie to Han, say that she spilled the sugar.

Hester knew too. How, Beulah couldn't work out. But she must have known, the way she went on, 'Did you see Louis's new suit, isn't it like something you'd see in a book!'

'What kind of a book?' snapped Beulah.

'Ah, you know what I mean.'

'Do I? Do I know what you mean? I do not, he looks like a fool.'

'His beard is getting long, now. Isn't it?'

'He's awful, he's, he's . . .' Beulah searched frantically, 'He's worse than Danny Fox,' and ran into the pantry to cram a tablespoon of demerara sugar into her mouth.

Unlike Bertie, Han didn't say much. But she was able to convey volumes through the expression of her eyes. And her eyes were telling Beulah that although she didn't believe Beulah's story about the toppling bag of sugar, she wasn't going to say anything about it. She handed Beulah her soft green purse, 'Just as well the rationing is over. Get another two-pound bag, I don't need as much as I thought I did before. I had a wealth of sour crab apples but I don't know where they've all gone.'

Hester jumped at her embroidery but Han didn't even look at her. 'Bertie will be disappointed, he said to me the other day that's what keeps him going through the winter, soda bread and crab apple jelly.'

Hester got up, 'There's a rake of them down below at Louis Kingston's. I know he'll let us have them. They never use them. They let them rot into the ground.'

Han came out of the store cupboard, 'Let Beulah go. She can call in to Louis's on her way back from the Cross.'

'I cannot, so I can't! I've a desperate sore leg!'

'Go on to the shop, let you. Give us a bit of peace.'

Beulah went out the back door, out of the silence, out of their white old-fashioned faces. Their big coils of hair balanced on the back of their necks. Just like her own hair was. Far too much of it, it was like a picture of a boa constrictor she'd seen in one of Louis's books. A boa constrictor was the length of six bicycles and it could wrap itself around a man and squeeze him to death.

Beulah ran all the way to the Cross and if her hair had fallen down she wouldn't have cared. Maybe she'd have been relieved, she wanted to let something go even if it was only her hair. But her hair didn't fall down. Han had it well secured with three long metal clips, heavy and solid. They could have been made by a blacksmith.

'Your breathing is bad, today, girleen,' said old Mrs Sheehan as Beulah stood panting at the counter. 'Are you wearing a strong knitted vest?'

'I was only running,' said Beulah but old Mrs Sheehan wasn't listening, she pulled out a long set of knitting needles attached to a yellowy white piece of knitting. 'I make three of these

92

every winter, since Nellie was born and there's never been as much as a squeak out of her chest.'

'We've strong chests, too,' Beulah said defensively.

There was a stigma attached to unhealthy families and it wasn't only Poleites, it was Catholics too. A distant cousin of the Sheehans had consumption and nobody knew a thing about it until she was brought out of the house in a coffin. The family were so ashamed. The infidels were in more danger, according to the Reverend Moylan, for they could get landed into hospital without warning. Old Mr Sheehan had died of lockjaw. Bertie had seen him being carted off to hospital with his jaw set and a trickle of blood running down the side of his mouth. 'To die away from his own and all belonging to him. Because God Almighty Dr Costello said so. How can that man sleep at night?' asked Bertie. 'They allow him every decision and he's not infallible.'

'Far from it,' said Han. 'Doesn't he drink?'

Han and Bertie had hung their heads the day Dr Costello drove into the yard with Beulah in the back seat, smelling perfume, leather, tobacco, shame and fear. Clutching her bag of brown sugar. There had been a smell of drink too. After she'd been sent to bed, Beulah heard Bertie and Han arguing about whether the smell of alcohol came from Dr Costello or his wife or both of them. Their voices reached into Beulah's and Hester's bedroom, unusually high-pitched.

'Of course, that's what it was, woman. You shouldn't have shook his hand.'

'I was only being neighbourly.'

'And what good will being neighbourly do you, when you're stone dead, laid out from disease? That man's a walking carpetbag of germs. Isn't he in and out of every sick house in the country, taking a drink everywhere of course. Do you think he washes his hands?'

93

'You know I'd give any one of them, the blackest infidel walking the road, the benefit of the doubt.'

'Oh Lord,' said Hester, sitting up in bed and putting her hands up to her face, 'I hope you didn't touch Joe Costello.'

'Get back to sleep, big ears!' hissed Beulah.

She was glad she didn't have to meet the Costellos at school. They were going back to their boarding schools after Easter. There was a time when it was the likes of Louis Kingston that went away to school but that was all changed now. Poleites! She hadn't minded them too much until she saw Louis turning into one.

When she'd been younger, at primary school, she'd hardly looked at Joe Costello, the infidel. Son of a doctor. Hester and Beulah had steered well out of his way and it hadn't been hard. Nobody tried too hard to be friends with the Kingstons. The other children had not found the Kingstons attractive. Their white faces, their long clothes, their sullen sitting silence all through the Angelus and every other prayer as well.

Of course, Hester hadn't been sullen always. Small Kay Carroll had been Hester's friend for a while. They'd been arm in arm around the yard with dandelion clocks and daisy chains and soldier weeds. Beulah didn't tell Bertie or Han, but Kay or someone must have told the Carrolls because the end came very quick. Overnight, in fact, Kay had come into school with her face turned away from Hester. Beulah told Hester to ignore her back, harder and it might have worked, she might have got Kay back that way. But Hester followed and followed Kay until Kay, feeling hounded, shouted at her to keep away. 'Aren't you only from a family of lunatics!' Well, it was clear to Beulah that Kay hadn't come up with that conclusion by herself, but Hester took the biggest offence in the end. 'We're the one true Christians!' she shouted back. 'And all of ye are going to Hell.'

A month later, Kay Carroll was attending the convent in the

town, because her father worked in town and it was handy. That was the reason given, but it must have been a consolation also to the Carrolls that there were no lunatics attending the convent.

Louis used to watch over them, helped them to build a Sultan's tent with twigs at the bottom of the school field. That took care of a lot of potentially lonely playtimes. The other children never went near the tent, at least not while Beulah, Louis and Hester were around. Whether it was out of fear or respect it was hard to say. It was never damaged, anyway, only rotted away during very wet weather soon after Louis left school.

Louis was a few years ahead and he'd left school early to help his father. Beulah heard Bertie complain to Han, 'That boy has brains, but Old Louis won't allow them to develop. He wants him at home so he can be leaning on him. There's nothing at all wrong with his old chest, nothing that a good clatter across the back wouldn't cure. He only puts on that old heavy breathing.'

Louis's old father leant hard on Louis. Louis had done most of the farmwork since he was about ten. He drove the churns to the creamery before school, he milked the cows, he mended fences. Old Mr Kingston's eyes were full of cataracts, he *was* too blind to work. But it was the way he took Louis's help as his due, that galled Bertie. He hated people being taken for granted. 'Old Louis still thinks he's one of the gentry with plenty of money for hired help. He forgets that it's his own son he's working into the ground.

'The old man is blind and sickly, no one can make him work,' said Han.

Louis got the first shilling he ever received from his father the night before he left school. He took it out at break-time in the playground and showed it to Beulah and Hester. They never had pocket money, wouldn't even dream of going to Mrs Sheehan's shop just to buy sweets for themselves as other children did.

95

As soon as the lunch bell rang on Louis's last day, Louis led Beulah and Hester out the school gate and down to the Cross, where he bought them three-quarters of a pound of sweets. A quarter of acid drops, a quarter of clove rock and a quarter of bull's eyes.

Beulah and Hester didn't know if they were allowed or not, so they hid them under their bed and sucked one each, every night until their stocks ran out, never saying a word to Han or Bertie and starting guiltily every time the wind knocked against their window.

After Louis left, they were isolated in the playground. Beulah sat with Hester and hopelessly tried to remember stories from *The Arabian Nights' Entertainments*. She couldn't even remember the end of Sinbad the Sailor's first voyage. Once or twice, Beulah caught Hester giving a longing glance at the girls playing hopscotch. There were still some girls that Hester was half inclined to talk to and that were half inclined to talk to Hester but Beulah never gave them a chance.

'Don't let that Kay Carroll kind of business happen ever again. How could you give them the say of it! We don't care a fig for the lot of them. We have Shep, we have Louis when we go home. We have Han and Bertie. They can whistle to the wind and turn fifty cartwheels but we will not look at them.'

'We have Louis,' said Hester and seemed comforted. But in her last year at primary school, Beulah met Joe Costello. And from that day when Joe listened to her heart with his father's stethoscope, Beulah didn't want to think about Louis anymore.

It came near to the time for Beulah's wedding and Beulah couldn't get it out of her head that it should be Hester getting married to Louis. Hester was the one who liked him, she was the good one. Even their names matched. Beulah couldn't understand why Han and Bertie weren't making a match

96

between Hester and Louis. Then she thought maybe they just hadn't noticed. She would have to tell them herself.

Beulah often touched the bony projection at the side of her wrist, it was a secret. The beautiful word she whispered to herself when she was all alone. *Styloid process*. It sounded smart. 'Look at that for style,' Nellie Sheehan always said about Margaret Costello. There could be no harm anyway in naming the parts of the body. It wasn't as if she was *taking* any medicine. She turned over her wrist and looked at the inside, the blue veins running across, diagonally. Blue blood as opposed to the bright red arterial blood. The dangerous blood full of oxygen. Bertie used the word oxygen to describe drunks. Staggering men with open singing mouths, they'd seen them from the trap on trips to town. 'Too much oxygen, by Jove!' said Bertie and cracked the whip to get away before Beulah could hear what the oxygenated men were shouting after them. *Oxygen, arterial, styloid process, lateral malleolus*. She wanted Joe to tell her more, to show her with his white hands. She didn't know how this could happen, but Louis was bound to be in her way.

One night when Han was on her own in the kitchen straining boiled fruit through a muslin cloth, Beulah crept downstairs to talk to her mother. Their house was poky, an eighteenth-century farmhouse with low ceilings, the girls' bedroom close enough to hear everything from the kitchen. Beulah could hear the drip of the fruit purée into the enamel bowl and Han's sighs as clear as Hester's quiet breathing.

She was sure by now that Han was sympathetic. Han had not scolded Beulah for all the mistakes and messes she had been making recently with her cooking, baking and sewing. Cakes burned, sauces curdled, stitches puckered beyond repair. Han never said one word. And so, Beulah was hoping that not only was Han sorry for her but she might even help.

Bertie had gone out earlier, visiting the Reverend Moylan's.

97

He was going to be late, he said and looked at Han. 'Louis Kingston could well be there tonight as well,' he said and gave an important cough. Han glanced at Beulah's face as he spoke.

Beulah continued to feel hopeful. That was why she didn't even obey the Poleite rules as she crept down the stairs in her long white nightgown. Shep was by the fire, she groaned with happiness as Beulah landed on the bottom step.

'Beulah! You gave me a terrible start. What's wrong? Are you ill?'

'No.'

'What are you doing down here dressed like that?'

'Dada won't be home for hours yet.'

'You don't know that and the Lord sees you. I see you.'

'But I'm completely covered.'

'In a flimsy nightgown, tonight! Preserve us!'

'It's as thick as wood, this cotton, I wouldn't call it silk now.' Beulah faltered, hearing the hard note in Han's voice. She knew now that her idea was not a good idea but it was too late to turn back.

'No, it's not silk, thank the Lord and what is gone wrong with you? I thought that you were afraid of getting married but now I don't know what's wrong with you.'

'I am afraid of getting married,' said Beulah.

'I'm glad you've told me, girl,' said Han, but her face and her gestures were not kind as she pushed Beulah into a seat. 'Wait until I get you my overcoat and I'll heat some milk for you.'

Beulah shivered but it wasn't the cold that made her shiver, it was the purposeful way that Han went to the press for her heavy tweed coat, the way she handled the heavy aluminium saucepan, silent and relentless like the wheels of a machine in a dream. A machine that would crush you and call it duty or kindness.

And Beulah and Han talked about duty and kindness, especially kindness to Bertie and Louis. 'They're only men after all, you have to take pity on them. They're afraid of sickness and death, they need to be held up.'

Was Han not afraid of death and sickness herself? Beulah sipped the hot milk. She pulled the collar of Han's dark coat around her chin, nervously as her mother misinterpreted (deliberately or not, she couldn't be sure) every qualm of Beulah's.

'But wouldn't it be better for Hester? She's the one who . . .'

'No, it would not be better. First and foremost and most importantly, your father wants to see you settled first. He is most anxious about it. You are the eldest and anyway, it's you that Louis likes. Does what Louis wants count with you at all?'

Han felt for her hairclips and began to reposition them one by one in her heavy coil of hair. Beulah watched each dark steel point disappear into the soft mass. 'I don't know where you've picked up this self-sacrificing idea, as if you were a Catholic.'

'I'm not self-sacrificing,' said Beulah, thinking that it was the marrying of Louis that would be the sacrifice.

'You must be feeling bad about all the pinches you were giving Hester,' Han dug another clip in so fast, Beulah was sure she'd break skin. 'Don't think that I didn't know all about that.'

Beulah was sure if Han knew all about the pinches, she must know the real truth of Beulah's feelings. If that was the case then Han was only pretending to think that Beulah's doubts were purely unselfish ones. Han pressed her hands against her head and pushed the bowl of fruit purée down to the other end of the table. What *was* she making? Beulah scanned the table for any sugar lying around. There was none.

'Child,' said Han. 'You're making me uneasy. Would you ever go up and put on your clothes, like a good girl. Come down then and I'll talk to you about marriage.'

Beulah staggered a bit in the dark, putting on her long dark stockings. Her legs felt heavy and her head and even her hands. What did she want to talk about marriage for? She didn't want to know what she was supposed to do. Whatever it was she wasn't going to do it anyway. Away from Han and Bertie, in Louis's house, she would do what she wanted. As much as she could manage, with life being so unfair. She looked at Hester, with her fair hair in a stiff bush on the pillow, her quiet breathing, her lipless mouth like a sheep's, Beulah felt a pang of loneliness. It surprised her. Beulah checked the buttons on her dress carefully, determined not to give Han any more chances to criticise.

Lying on the hospital trolley, Beulah fingered the buttons of her blue dress, the man with the bow legs had fallen silent. Sheila Sheehan was preparing to go away. 'I would like to have seen you into the room . . .' Beulah interrupted, 'Where is Hester? Why isn't she here? Everyone else has their relatives with them.'

Sheila looked at the bow-legged man, 'And what's wrong with this grand little man to keep you company?'

The little man smoothed back his few wisps of hair, delightedly.

'I want my sister.' Beulah tried to turn her head away, but the hard collar wouldn't let her.

The door opened and Mrs Treadle came out, 'Come on now, Beulah!' She motioned to Nurse Bolton to grab hold of the trolley as she steered it expertly through the doorway.

'If you're going to casualty, tell them I need a doctor to pull down the arms!' Mrs Treadle shouted out to Sheila and Sheila shouted back that she was going there to get Hester. 'They were always devoted, the two creatures,' Sheila announced, generally, talking about Beulah and Hester as if they were dead. Beulah remembered that there had been a time when Sheila had been half afraid of her, when she had been full of respect, *Yes, Mrs Kingston and No, Mrs Kingston. Seven big bottles of Seven-Up? Certainly, Mrs Kingston, and would you like a little box to carry them?*

The voices went like shuttlecocks over and back across the trolley, 'You see, I have to have the arms pulled down otherwise we won't see the first cervical spine,' Mrs Treadle was saying to Sheila Sheehan.

'They're not *the* arms, they're *my* arms,' Beulah said.

'Now, love,' said Mrs Treadle, throwing her own tanned arms around Beulah. 'We know you're frightened.'

'I am not frightened!' said Beulah, her ears picking up the sound of Hester's rubber soles, which stuck and squeaked and wrenched along the shiny hospital floors.

'What kept you!' she said, her heart battering her chest with the relief of seeing her sister. Beulah hadn't noticed, until now, how old and bent Hester had become.

'Do you want to come in?' Mrs Treadle asked Hester. 'Come on in here behind the control panel, you'll be safe out.' Mrs Treadle ushered Hester behind the control panels where Hester kept smiling at Mrs Treadle.

Hester had always been partial to glamour. Joe Costello's sister Margaret, for example; Hester had spent years talking about Margaret's suits, those suits that nearly finished Reverend Moylan, with their short tight skirts, their tiny jackets. Herringbone tweed, light-green summer ones, and of course the mustard one. Hester had only caught a glimpse of the mustard suit one day as Margaret was getting into her car to drive into town. Her curiosity piqued, Hester got the bus into town. Following, to get a better look. It was the only time that Hester had given Han and Bertie cause for concern.

Hester was gone for hours while Bertie roamed the fields with a pitchfork, convinced that she had been abducted. Han even went as far as the Cross and humiliated herself, asking Nellie Sheehan if she had seen where Hester had gone.

Hester came back in the evening, slipping quietly into the kitchen, her eyes lowered in front of Bertie and Han. Bertie and Han were astounded that Hester could have forgotten her hat.

Hester's face was crimson with sunburn, her nose like a beacon, after standing for an hour in the noonday sun, waiting for the bus. It was like a rash of embarrassment and repentance, yet Beulah knew that Hester wasn't sorry. Hester would risk anything to know more about sewing or materials.

'There isn't one ounce of shade on that main road,' Bertie moaned, 'it's not just the immodesty of it, it's your health, your health. You've nothing if you haven't got your health!'

Han said, 'Well, you and your strawberry-coloured thread, you are an out-and-out perfectionist!'

Hester was let off far more lightly than Beulah herself would have been. Beulah seethed and hated Hester, but later in the evening, she was afraid that Hester might be suffering from slight sunstroke, as she muttered half asleep, '. . . had to see them. Lord, they were beautiful buttons, two-tone, you know. Yellow swirling into brown and the shape of them! Round with a hint of oval. Would that suit have ever come from Paris?' Beulah gave her a shake, 'Shh, can't you? Dada will hear!'

Mrs Treadle was Margaret Costello's niece, she had that same blonde glamour. An air of riches. Mrs Treadle, with her high glossy black patent pumps, toeless and backless, clinging effortlessly by virtue of Mrs Treadle's high instep. How did she manage them with all the walking around that she had to do? Mrs Treadle could have been a circus performer, the way she clicked around the room, lifting the weighty protective apron onto Dr Kumar's shoulders and whizzing the ceiling-suspended X-ray camera around the room to focus on Beulah's prostrate neck. She balanced a steel plate on the other side of Beulah, propping it up with sandbags and boxes of tissues and anything else that came to her beautifully manicured hand.

Beulah could see Hester craning her neck around the side of the control panel, to get a better look at Mrs Treadle as she worked. Joe's mother had been the first woman that they had ever seen with red nails. Beulah said they made her sick, they

102

were predatory-looking, 'Horrible talons, like a beast of prey would have! Don't they remind you, Hester, of that fierce orc bird in "Sinbad the Sailor"?'

But Hester was no longer interested in *The Arabian Nights*, she said that she loved red nails. Han and Bertie never knew how Hester was taken up with vanities. Although Beulah would never dream of telling them, it annoyed her that they didn't know. It was Joe Costello who noticed Beulah's virtues. *I like natural girls*.

Chapter Ten

Beulah and Louis's wedding was full of light. Sunbeam upon sunbeam streamed everywhere, on the empty glasses stacked up waiting for lemonade, the polished table, Hester's fair hair, The Reverend Moylan's black suit, gleaming with crystals of spilt sugar.

Worried about his strength before such a momentous ceremony, Han had made the Reverend Moylan sit down at the end of the kitchen table (its oilskin cloth discarded for the day and replaced with white damask linen) to drink tea with honey and eat her own lemon cake.

'You're an important man, we can't have you falling down on the ground!'

'Mrs Kingston, I'm bowing to you out of politeness! Let us go into the parlour and pray that the war will soon be over.'

But it wasn't so much the end of the war, it was the end of rationing for which the Reverend was praying. He swept into the parlour, his blood roaring with sugar, to conduct a service that included such passionate renditon of psalms, that Bertie broke out clapping and had to be pinched by Han.

It was mostly the Reverend Moylan that Beulah remembered from the wedding. Everyone else, including the bride and groom, had taken a back seat. He was the liveliest person there, in fact, he was probably the most lively Poleite in existence. He knew it too. He revelled in it, roaring, stormily, THE LORD IS MY SHEPHERD! And then, in a low, low emotional voice whispering *Thou preparest a table before me in the presence of mine enemies*. Thanking Han with the words of the Bible. And if he extended King David's lyrics into *Thou hast fed my lips with lemon cake over snow-white linen*, would any of them have even noticed, the way he had them all so mesmerised?

Beulah sneaked a few looks at Louis's dark besotted face. It was hard to do because Louis was continually trying to peer under the awkward angles of his hat at Beulah. So most of the time, Beulah looked at his round-toed black shoes, the gleam of them! He must have been up half the night, she hoped that he had spent hours on them, that he had lost sleep over them. He'd want to be clean now.

'You must not let Louis look upon your naked body and you must not look upon his.' Han steadily avoided Beulah's horrified look and steadily produced the pile of sheets they had to hem for the wedding. Six pairs.

'Keep a sheet between you at all times!'

There would be no need for that, Beulah thought, as she sewed away. There were plenty of bedrooms in Louis Kingston's house, no need for them to share at all. Beulah had always hated sewing, it gave her a crick in her neck. Hemming was full of carefulness and boredom. Han ripped out any stitch that was the slightest bit crooked.

The wedding dress was made and ironed and hanging in Han's big wardrobe. It was a masterpiece, they all agreed. Hester had been allowed to design it and make the most of it, even though Beulah should really have made it all herself. It was full length of course, made of soft dark grey wool. It had a high neck and not too fitted. Hester had picked the lightest woollen material, it felt like silk. At least what Beulah imagined silk would feel like, Beulah had never even touched silk, it was not a Poleite material. Palest of pale grey lace for the collar; Hester had been allowed to get lace and it had been more of a concession to Hester's artistic vision than it was to Beulah's wedding dress. Two pearl buttons on the cuff of each long sleeve and that was it. Yet it hung and fitted her body like a soft floating dream that made Beulah feel beautiful. She walked out of her bedroom, balancing her heavy, plaited crown of hair like a queen, wishing that Joe Costello could see her looking so natural.

Wild hopeless dreams occupied Beulah for most of the day; Joe arriving at the farm with an urgent message, cows escaped from the fort field or some other catastrophe. Joe arriving at the moment when Reverend Moylan asked if anyone knew any reason why Louis Giles Kingston should not be joined with Beulah May Kingston. Weren't their names enough of an indication that it was wrong? Surely they must be related if you went back far enough? Beulah couldn't even bear to think of Louis as her brother anymore. All that week coming up to the wedding, Beulah had nightmares about Louis smothering her with sheets.

In *The Arabian Nights* reluctant brides were downcast, prostrate, they tore their hair and swooned. Beulah didn't experience these waves, she was hemmed in, yet she felt hopelessly hopeful. She patted her stiff crown and fingered a piece of her fine wool dress. One half of her expected Joe to burst in the door at any moment while the other half knew very well that this was the most private of weddings of the most private of private sects. Even Danny Fox, Louis's friend and farming advisor would not dare to pass through the yard. Beulah would go back with Louis to the house by the stream where she had longed to live as a child. Where she had longed to live with Louis as her brother, listening to the water-wheel as it turned and turned. *Alf Layla wa Layla! One Thousand and One Nights.*

106

High tea was the greatest feast for Poleites and Han had been preparing for months. The autumn before, special jars had been put to one side. Homemade strawberry, gooseberry, blackcurrant and rhubarb jam, crab apple jelly. Han bottled her own pickled onions, beetroot and cauliflower. For weeks now, Han, Hester and Beulah had been baking fruit cakes and madeira cakes. Gingerbread. Huge barm bracks like dairy cheeses sat in the pantry. The day before, they roasted ham, beef and lamb. They'd baked bread, white, wholemeal and soda. That morning they made the devilled eggs, stuffed tomatoes, lemonade and orangeade. All this, even though there were only six people for tea, Reverend Moylan, Bertie, Han, Beulah, Louis and Hester.

Beulah thought that Han was suffering from some form of wedding madness and she had expected Bertie to intervene and put a halt to it all, but Bertie was worse than Han. 'Whatever you do, don't use those mangy pullet eggs, get the big brown ones, even if you have to go down to Mrs Sheehan. You better have a Victoria sponge for the Reverend as well, and don't forget to press it upon him. The poor man needs it, he has to be stopped from trying the impossible.'

The Reverend Moylan had never been so extrovert, dashing about the farmhouse, his coat swinging, complimenting Bertie on his smart fencing, Han on her cooking, Hester on her sewing, Beulah and Louis on their modesty because he could think of nothing else to say about them. At least that's what Beulah thought and she didn't know how they could all look upon the Reverend so solemnly while he patted Louis's shoulder, saying 'Modest man, modest man,' over and over with Louis grinning like a goblin, darting sidelong glances at Beulah.

Beulah knew that they were all expecting her to blush when she was led out to the pony and trap at seven o'clock. Louis was blushing enough for the both of them, his face like a lighthouse going on and off as he bent over their wedding present, Sally, a jet black pony, that Bertie had bought for them to pull the trap.

Beulah wouldn't have blushed anyway but she could feel herself white with anger as the wedding party stood outside the parlour window, waving them off cheerfully. As if it was Beulah's own idea to go off on this jaunty ride with Louis when the truth of it was that she had not one single say in the whole event from start to finish.

The evening was getting cool when they clopped in over the cobbles, Shep sitting up straight as a die, behind Beulah. Sunset streaks of pink and orange lined up over the roof as Beulah stood under the galvanised canopy outside the pantry listening to the sounds of the stream. Beulah looked up at the old house. She would get this place to her own clean satisfaction. She would sweep away everything, all the traces of lazy Old Louis Kingston, it was *her* house, now, to do what she wanted. And she would do what she wanted, whatever Louis was thinking, coming across the cobbles with his old-man's gait, his red face going on and off.

'After you,' Louis said to Beulah, with a sweep of his hand. Beulah went down the stone steps ahead of him, her plait of hair heavy on her head. They passed through the milky-smelling scullery, Beulah could hear Louis's breathing, she did not dare to look back. She wished she wasn't wearing such fine grey wool, the way it clung to her back. Was she perspiring? After what seemed a very long time, her feet touched the flagged floor of the kitchen and Louis cried out in despair.

'What is it?' Beulah asked without turning around.

'A mistake,' said Louis.

Beulah still didn't look around, 'It *was* a mistake,' she began.

'Ah, no! I've let you down. Badly!'

'Well, it's a bit late now!'

'No, I won't let it so,' said Louis, as hope leapt inside Beulah. 'Gimme your hand.' She felt his hard warm palm in hers, she

108

tried to pull away but he pulled harder, 'Look, here to me.'

She turned her head on its damp neck, like someone afraid to look at a new wound when the bandage is first removed. Louis was there, looking much the same as always. He seemed smaller than before but then he'd grown so large in her imagination during the journey down the steps and into the kitchen, anyone would seem smaller. The same pale blue eyes, wispy beard and loose black suit.

Louis was unsure and very determined at the same time. 'We can go out and come back in again.'

'What are you talking about, Louis?'

Louis pulled at her hand, 'We can go out and come back in again, forget that I brought you in this way.'

'Are you gone clean mad?'

'I know I am a fool, I was too happy to think of the front door. You know we never used it and that was part of the problem. Come on Beulah, I won't be right until I bring you back in the front way.' There were tears like rocks of crystal in his blue eyes, 'I'm sure that it's fierce unlucky to come in the back door.'

'All right, so!' Beulah exclaimed, mad with pity. 'But I'm not holding your hand.'

'I know I don't deserve it,' Louis hung his head. 'But maybe you'll hold my hand when I get you inside the right way.'

'Go on then!' said Beulah as Louis led the way swiftly through the pantry. Darkness had begun to fall in the yard, bits of machinery and churns crouched, ivy swayed. Louis and Beulah went out of the cobbled yard and past the tall wrought-iron gates to the front of the house. The house looked bigger and grander from this side. It wasn't cluttered with the veranda and outhouses the way the back was, Louis creaked at the lock for a few minutes and Shep, who had followed like a shadow, began to bark. At first the gates wouldn't give way.

'I wouldn't be surprised if this wasn't used since my mother died,' Louis said.

Beulah didn't want to hear about Louis's mother, 'We'll feel stupid having to go round again,' she shrugged. 'Shep will think that we are stone mad.' As if she was waiting to be mentioned, Shep ran up and began sniffing the new wool of Beulah's dress. Beulah touched Shep's head, she was scared of the place now, so different in the night, 'Please can we go back,' she whispered as the gate creaked open.

Louis led the way this time. Triumphant. 'There's nothing wrong with those gates that a bit of 3-IN-ONE oil won't put right. They'll be oiled from this out, I'm telling you.'

Beulah followed. The darkness had come quick as if someone had thrown a dark blanket over the two of them in their new home. They were buried, forgotten about. Louis was eighteen and she was barely seventeen. What did they know about running a house, let alone a farm, together?

Louis was confident enough, now, moving around in the dark hall. He found the lantern, struck a match and the old musty hall filled with light. Beulah saw piles of dust, cobwebs, scuffs on the wainscot, but she did not comment. Louis was like a small black spider scurrying down the passage ahead of her, she knew that she couldn't deliberately hurt him.

'Well, now,' said Louis and as he heaved it onto the table, Beulah realised that he had been carrying a basket in his left hand the whole time. It was one of Han's, brown with age and wear, straws sticking out of one side. 'There's a fair share of sweet cake inside here, will you have a bit while I make the tea?'

Beulah was about to refuse when she remembered the new sheets that had already been installed upstairs by Han, during the week. 'I'm thirsty for tea, have you any ordinary white sugar?'

Louis went to the old painted press and took out a brown bag of sugar. The sight of the brown bag made Beulah think of Joe and she glared resentfully at Louis as he made his way out to the scullery to fill the kettle. She went to the drawer of the press, noticing as she did so the thickness and freshness of the salmon pink paint. Louis must have applied the last awkward, drippy coat in preparation for her arrival. Inside the drawer was a tablespoon which she dipped into the bag of sugar, hurriedly. Louis came back in to ask a question and found her with the spoon to her lips and crystals of sugar clinging to her cheeks, her neck, the collar of her dress.

'Are you that hungry?' he asked her.

'I am,' Beulah said and dug into the brown paper bag again.

'What about the limon cake?'

'It is lemon not limon, you're starting to talk like Danny Fox,' Beulah sprayed the air with sugar. 'And stop looking like that, there is nothing wrong with you!'

'Looking like what?' asked Louis.

'Like a dog who's lost his bone.'

There was a silence while Beulah crammed her mouth with more sugar, crunching was the only sound apart from the solemn tick-tock of the brown clock over the couch by the range. Louis turned away, a sorry black-suited sight in the doorway as he lowered his head to go through into the scullery. Beulah kept cramming and cramming the sugar. She was free, free, free. No Bertie or Han to tell her what to do. Only Louis and he was afraid because he liked her too much. On the Stanley range the kettle was stirring, Louis was scalding the teapot. Beulah thought, in that moment, how she was freer than many of the women infidels in the town with their pinch-waisted suits and their makeup and high heels. She had her own house and her own sugar.

Louis came in with the tea.

'I'm afraid there isn't a speck of sugar left,' Beulah said. 'I'm still growing.' She began to feel a bit bad now. She was talking to Louis's bowed shoulders.

'I don't take sugar,' he said.

They drank their tea silently while Beulah wondered if maybe it was pity and not submissiveness that was bowing his shoulders. The lemon cake sat on a china plate like a rebuke from Han. 'Why don't you appreciate Louis? Why can't you eat sweet cake like a normal human being instead of going around with your head in a brown bag of sugar like a horse with a bag of oats!'

He couldn't make her sleep with him, could he? She wasn't used to it. How could anyone expect her to? But Louis was nervous too, she could see by the way he fidgeted with his beard like a nervous young girl adjusting her hair.

The staircase was dark with old wood, painted brown. The stairs creaked, the carpet was wafer thin with knobby brass rails holding frayed and broken bits down. 'Mind your step,' said Louis. Beulah followed him.

On the first landing, Louis threw open a dark door. 'Mama's room.' He waited, expecting her to go in ahead. Beulah paused in the doorway, there was a big lumpy-looking bed with iron ends and a heavy coverlet of some rusty material that could have passed for a type of iron itself. 'Can I sleep anywhere I like?' she asked timidly, afraid of her own shadow, which was thrown across the dark panelling, a huge-nosed crone.

'Han came up here with a fright of sheets during the week, she did three different rooms for us.'

'Us?'

'Who else, but us. Now, there's a kind of a triangle-shaped room down here at the end of the passage. Grand-uncle Georgie's. And upstairs there's my own room. It is bright in the morning or even if you've got the right night, the moon gives a great blast of light.'

'But it's sleeping we want to be!' Beulah broke in.

'Well, down here the passage, we better go for the triangle room.'

Uncle Georgie's room had a lot of books even though there

112

were many more marks and empty spaces on the shelves, indicating the ones that had been taken away. Bertie said that he, Georgie Kingston, had been notorious for reading dangerous books. The Poleite minister who converted the Kingstons had spent a whole night crying out to the heavens, as he flicked through the pages between the covers. There was a bonfire late in the evening when the minister threw dozens of books into the flames. 'What books were they?' Beulah had asked when Bertie was telling her.

'Oh, child don't ask! And sure even if I knew I couldn't tell you because I didn't ask myself. I'd imagine they were by the worst people possible.'

'Who are they? The worst people?' asked Beulah.

'I'd say the very worst now and I could be wrong, but I'd say I'm right that the very worst ones are the Catholics that have turned atheist.'

Beulah had wanted to ask what were atheists but Bertie went on, 'To give Old Louis his due, though, he forbade that minister to destroy a lot of others, Alfred Lord Tennyson and William Morris, he was a good man.'

'What are atheists?' Beulah asked Louis, now on the threshold of Old Georgie's room.

Louis looked surprised at the question but he did know. 'They are people with no religion at all, they're not Lutherans or Methodists, or Pagans or Catholics.'

Beulah wondered was she an atheist. The way she got bored with the Reverend Moylan and the Bible.

Louis said, 'Don't tell a soul, but I think Uncle Georgie was one.' He caught hold of her hand again and Beulah didn't shake him off as they walked up to Georgie's bed. 'You're my wife now, we can tell each other everything. The Reverend Moylan said every man needs a woman to tell things to. He said that he tells everything to Han, that she's the guardian of his health. He was over here a month ago and he had a fierce feed of honey that seemed to loosen his tongue. I didn't mind at all, I'd an awful lot to find out.'

'I don't think I want to sleep here after all,' Beulah said. 'Where is your room?'

Louis led the way up an even narrower, darker set of stairs, stopping at an old sliding door. He braced himself, having to lift the door on its hinges in order for it to crash back along its rails. 'A divil of a door,' he gasped and Beulah didn't want to remind him that he was talking like Danny Fox again as he added, 'mind out the steps.'

Three deep steps led into Louis's room. It was a deep queer shape like a well tucked onto the house sideways. The ceiling was low, whitewashed and there were three raggedy books on the bedside locker.

'There's great heat here,' Beulah said and Louis showed her the gleaming copper pipes that came up from the kitchen, 'Do you know, I'm glad you're going for this room. It's the warmest of all.'

Louis's bed was huge like the iron bed but it was more beautiful, with inlaid mahogany bed ends. Beulah paused to admire it. 'I moved my mother's bed in here, I was hoping that you'd go for this room on account of the heat and all. Han gave me a hand the other night because I was afraid I'd damage the woodwork if I did it on my own. The minute Louis mentioned Han's name, Beulah threw back the magenta eiderdown and there were the sheets she had resentfully hemmed.

Keep a sheet between the two of ye at all times!

'I prefer iron beds.' Beulah had a shake in her voice, she nearly fell up the three steps in her hurry to get out. 'What about the moonlight in your mother's room?'

'Hold your whist,' said Louis as he tried to get control of the sliding door off her. 'You don't know how to handle her.'

'Who?' said Beulah.

'The door.'

'You shouldn't be calling it a "her". You only picked that up from Danny Fox, he is so ignorant, he even calls the horse's bridle a she.'

'There's no harm in it.'

'But you're not a fool like Danny Fox. Have you forgotten that you're a Kingston, who had money and standing when nobody around here had it.'

'That's not a Christian way to be looking at things.'

'But sure there's no such thing as Christian! There's only Poleite, Calvinist, Catholic or Pagan! Anyway, I'm sure that it is a sin to call everything a woman,' Beulah trembled as Louis had laid his hand on her arm. 'Will you let me out of this box of a place!'

The two of them traipsed back through the corridors, Beulah could hear Shep whining with fright down below in the kitchen. Her head ached and she felt a tickle in her throat. She coughed but it wouldn't go. She continued to cough as she followed Louis into the bedroom.

'A glass of water might settle you,' Louis said, pouring from the jug on the dressing table. Beulah drank and her cough went. Louis left to get undressed in another room.

Chapter Eleven

When Louis came back, he got under the covers quick, pulling them up until they almost covered his head. He stuck out his work-callused hand and groped around the top of the bedside locker for the old tin alarm clock. His eyes peeped over the top of the eiderdown, they were such a strange pale blue, powder blue Hester might have called them. Hester learned all her colours in the draper's shop: China blue, Indigo, Forget-Me-Not, Slate, Gunmetal grey, Donkey brown.

With his beard under the covers, Louis looked very young, 'Cripes! Is that the time?' he said, and she knew that he was talking like Danny Fox now on purpose. She closed her eyes and heard him rattle the clock as he put out the light. 'Well, isn't that a fright! I forgot the light.' She heard his bare feet thud on the lino and she didn't want to think about what his bare legs and feet might look like. She clenched her eyelids tighter. The light went off, the room hummed with warmth and silence.

'G'night,' said Louis and turned over.

He didn't snore. He had light breathing like a child's. Beulah felt like a child herself, sitting up and willing him to wake up because she didn't know the sounds of the house yet. The copper pipes twanged and Beulah imagined ghosts, all standing up on top of each other like pictures she'd seen on posters for the circus. Long thin athletic spirits, creeping their skinny fingers all the way up the copper pipes.

After what seemed like hours, she got out of bed and went around to Louis's side to look at the clock. It was eleven o'clock, Beulah had never been up that late before. She went over to the window and tore back the curtains, trying to wake up Louis. There was very little moonlight but the curtains were noisy moving on the brass rail. Louis slept on while Beulah caught hold of the curtains, gave them a vicious sweep shut again. Still Louis slept on. As she got back into bed, Beulah wondered who could possibly haunt the place.

Beulah could barely remember Louis's mother. It had been a long time since she had gone to her funeral with Han and Bertie and seen Mrs Kingston's strange body laid out in Louis's parlour. The corpse was like something that had been made out of putty and then dyed bright yellow. Mrs Kingston's hair was parted in the middle, the thin yellow line of the parting running razor sharp and straight through her jet black hair.

Mrs Fox, Danny's mother, had been on her feet then and Beulah remembered her saying to Han, 'Hasn't she got desperate black hair?' and Han saying with a tremble in her voice, 'She's only young, sure, she's not even forty.'

Beulah had tried to ask Bertie about some things that she didn't understand. And Bertie had refused to explain, only patted her cheek and her head so much that Han had to tell him to stop. 'You're making a pure show of yourself.' Beulah thought that there had been a kind of thin green netting like the netting from a shopping bag only much larger of course, spread over the body but she couldn't be sure. It was a long time ago.

Then, out of the blue, lying there in Louis's bed with her knees pulled up uncomfortably to her chin, Beulah recalled another earlier memory of Louis's mother.

One dark winter evening, ten-year-old Beulah had been sent by Han with a message for old Mr Kingston. Some message that

117

Reverend Moylan had written down on a piece of blue lined notepaper. He hadn't time to deliver it himself, he said, and his eyebrows had worked up and down when he gave the note to Han. 'It's imperative that Mr Louis Kingston gets it tonight.'

Beulah's stomach crept with fear when Han said, 'Beulah will take it down now, she's as steady as they go. She'll see that it gets there all right.'

Han took down Beulah's dark heavy coat and held it out for Beulah to slip her arms into the sleeves. Beulah looked at the dark gathering outside the window. Hadn't her mother noticed how windy, how gloomy it was out there? Her mother pulled up her hood, 'Don't speak to any infidels and hold this message tight.'

'Will she be all right in the dark?' the Reverend asked, and Beulah paused hopefully.

'Beulah's afraid of nothing, she's the coolest customer I've ever met,' said Han, speaking as if she and Beulah were not even related. As if she was describing some outsider to Reverend Moylan.

The Reverend was impressed with Beulah. He called her intrepid. 'One of these days, now, I'll buy you a barley sugar twist.'

Han gave Beulah a basket with pots of jam and an empty bottle. 'Get young Louis to fill the bottle with fresh milk. We want half a dozen eggs as well. We're very short.'

Han pulled up her hood and followed her to the back door to whisper urgently into Beulah's ear, 'Give the message into Mr Kingston's hand and no one else's mind. If Mrs Kingston is there, she's too forgetful, anyhow you won't meet her, she is bedridden all the time now.'

Dark clouds rolled across the sky between the bare branches of the tree and a gust of wind blew the last few papery leaves. Beulah staggered against the gable end of the wall and clicked her tongue as Shep ran up.

But even Shep couldn't keep the gusts of fear at bay. They bowled along inside her stomach as fast as the dark clouds were bowling overhead. She began to run, but that seemed to make the trees wave faster and the air darker and so she stopped and crept along with Shep running ahead, and she wanted to call out to Shep to come back and stay near her. She needed the pressure of Shep's body against her legs, but she was afraid to call out.

Finally, she stood at the door, her knees weak with dread, the yard in darkness. She knocked timidly at first, but no one answered. The stream wasn't a friendly spirit now, it was guttural and fierce.

She knocked louder but no one answered. Why did Louis or George not answer? She felt there was some quiet listener standing behind the door, even though all she could hear was the stream, the clank of the water-wheel and Shep's impatient whines. She put down her basket and picked it up again, fearing some invisible grabbing hand. Shep began to lick the cobbled stones as if there were some traces of food or milk spilled on them. She raised her hand a third time and hammered with all her might, shouting wildly, 'I've come with a message for the Kingstons, is there anyone there at all?'

She had not finished shouting when she saw the latch yank upwards as it was released from the inside. Standing there was a woman with long hair falling down to her shoulders. Her yellow face was lined. It was shocking for Beulah to see the woman's hair hanging down. She wanted to look away.

At first she thought the woman was growling at her but then she realised the woman was trying to say, 'What is it?' It was as if her tongue or her teeth or something was missing from her mouth.

'It's a message from Reverend Moylan,' Beulah said, holding out the note at first and then pulling it back when she remembered her mother's warning.

'Is Mr Louis there?' Beulah said as the woman's hand came forward to take the note.

The woman shook her head from side to side, her yellow hand coming for the note.

Beulah put her hand behind her back. 'Where's Louis?' she asked.

Mrs Kingston muttered again and Beulah guessed that she was saying 'Give that here to me'.

She stood still, while Shep began to jump up and bark at the woman. The woman said some other words and Beulah knew that she was saying that she could trust her and Beulah felt pity so she gave the woman the note. She wanted to please the woman, to make her smile, but the woman only snatched the note when Beulah held it out. And with a triumphant look, proud of her own cunning and the way that she had got the note from Beulah, she slammed the door in Beulah's face.

Beulah ran all the way to the top of the avenue where she stopped when she realised that she hadn't got the milk or eggs. If she said that there was no one at Kingston's, then her mother would ask her for the letter. Beulah dragged her steps all the way home. But Han never asked about the note or the eggs or the milk. When Beulah got back, Hester was sick and Han was far too occupied with Hester. The Reverend Moylan never asked about the note either and Beulah gradually forgot all about the incident until now.

Beulah turned her hot pillow a thousand times. She buried her nose in the pillow, trying to smell the privet hedge where Han had dried the sheets. And then she thought about all the linen, the towels and the washing that was hers to do from now on. She thought about scrubbing the floors and the walls. And how she would have her very own washday, with beads of perspiration running down her face, like a proper married woman.

Chapter Twelve

Twice a week, Louis saddled up the trap and they drove the seven miles into town. Beulah got all her meat from the butcher's; chops, oyster cut of bacon, rib of beef. Now and then, Louis talked about killing a pig but she always talked him out of it.

It was a smart trap, Louis spent hours every Monday polishing the side brasses. Early Tuesday morning, they clopped down the main street and half the town came out to watch them. Such young newly-weds, in their strange black clothes, their white faces under their hats and Louis's thin beard swaying as he held the reins.

Louis and Beulah looked straight ahead with straight faces. Like royalty, they'd been used to attention from an early age. The townspeople were colder, more distant, and they weren't afraid to smirk in the presence of Poleites. Even as children, Beulah and Hester had copied their parents' stony faces, but Han often held her wrist too tight, or Bertie hit his pony too hard.

It was different at Two Mile Cross, where they were known. They were tolerated, even liked by most people, thanks to Old Mrs Sheehan, who never tired of saying how fond she was of all the Kingstons. 'Both sides of them, they're gentlemen and ladies to their fingertips. They come and go and mind their own business.'

'Bad business?' Danny Fox suggested. Even as a teenager, he had a fondness for hanging around where he wasn't wanted.

'If only my arms were longer, then I could give you a good clip around the ear! Get home to your mother, you young scut!'

It wasn't just Old Mrs Sheehan, there were others, the Kingstons always had champions and friends in the village, people who appreciated their hard work, their honesty. People who knew that any one of the Kingstons could be called upon to give a hand to a neighbour in trouble.

The townspeople didn't care and they were smarter, so they made the Poleites stand out even more. Nearly all the young women had perms, short skirts to just below their knee, high noisy heels. Some shop girls laughed at Beulah before she had even left a shop. There were corner Johnnies, with Woodbines between their lips, who muttered under their caps at Louis when he passed them on the street. He didn't like coming to town but Beulah was dead set on the butcher's for all her meat. Louis didn't know how to force her to make black puddings and sausages at home. Even if he knew how to force her, he wouldn't have wanted to.

Beulah hated the way the shop girls looked at her, the dowdy feel of the hem of her skirt touching her ankles. But Joe Costello was in town often, collecting drugs from the pharmacy to take to his father's surgery.

When Louis and Beulah had finished their shopping, they walked back to the trap, Beulah shivering with the lie she was about to say, 'Haven't I forgot the castor oil? Wait, here now and I won't be a minute!'

Afraid that Louis would object, say they had enough castor oil, or why could she not get it from Mrs Sheehan, Beulah ran away the minute she said it. She ran so quickly that she felt the huge roll of hair that she'd fixed at the back of her neck slip to one side. She pushed it back and slowed down, but it didn't feel secure. She wondered if she should go back to Louis. Hesitating for a moment, she turned back to see Louis sitting up at the front of the trap, watching her. He gave a friendly wave and she felt now that she couldn't turn back. He might get suspicious. She walked more slowly, her head held stiffly. Outside the chemist shop, she fidgeted with the buttons of her coat.

The bell jangled as she entered. Joe didn't seem to be there and she was only half disappointed. She was as much afraid of meeting him as she was longing to see him. She had thought far too much about him, put her finger too often on her styloid process, she wouldn't be comfortable or casual meeting him now. As she gazed around, her mouth fell open. Mortified, she snapped it shut so hard she bit her tongue. Dizzy with pain, she sniffed the smell of lemons, lavender, roses. Such a clean place. Such beautiful mahogany and glass-fronted cases. The mysterious bottles and prescriptions behind the counter that were forbidden to Poleites. As were the cosmetics. Creams and potions that made women as beautiful as the faces on the pictures smiling around the shop. There was a tiny bottle marked 1s. 3d, filled with a clear liquid called 'Ashes of Roses'. As Beulah leant down to pick the bottle up, she felt someone gently touch her hair.

Joe Costello looked half ashamed, but he didn't step backwards. He was near enough for Beulah to make out the green flecks in his brown eyes. 'I could see your hair was about to fall, if I didn't push that hairclip right in.'

Beulah couldn't answer him. But the woman from behind the counter spoke up. 'The whole lot is going to collapse anyway, if it isn't fixed in the next few minutes. Come in here, behind, to me and I'll get you out of the eye of the public.'

Mrs Tobin, another doctor's wife, ran the chemist's shop. She made up the prescriptions and tied the cosmetics in pretty parcels. She was not conventional, but very kind. Beulah didn't know this so she followed her in to the back room. Joe knew she was unconventional. He followed them both.

123

'Mind the step,' called Mrs Tobin, as she bustled ahead; she was an elegant-looking woman, her grey blonde hair piled high over a beautiful plump face with a silvery blonde fringe.

Mrs Tobin wore a midnight-blue dress and pearls, her matching blue heels were high. To stop herself staring at Mrs Tobin and to avoid looking at Joe, who was staring at her, Beulah scrutinised the back room. A funny place. More cabinets displaying large blue glass bottles full of medicines and smaller glass cups and jugs lying around. 'Pharmacy is a kind of a witchcraft, if you like,' the Reverend Moylan said. 'Drugs distilled and created from plants and the Lord knows what. At least, before, the people had some kind of an idea, at least they would know what a name might mean. They would know that belladonna was deadly nightshade, that opium and laudanum came from the poppy. They might stay clear then, if they had an ounce of sense.'

Beulah stared around Mrs Tobin's inner sanctum. The middle of one wall was almost completely taken up with a huge carved mahogany fireplace. The mantelpiece had a clock and a couple of dusty Dresden figures, the tips of their pink delicate fingers, their dusky pink dresses barely visible behind all the letters and papers that were piled up in front of them. Two soft armchairs stood in front of the fire and along the adjacent wall, there was a long leatherette couch with buttons embedded in its back.

'Sit down here, child,' said Mrs Tobin. 'And let me get at your head, you're fierce tall altogether.'

Beulah sat down. Louis sitting up, waiting on the trap, was just a vague picture at the back of her mind. It was not troubling her too much at the moment. Joe wore brown suede gaiters. He was a qualified doctor now and he rode his horse around the countryside making calls. Leaving the car to his father who was getting old.

All that was needed was a couple more hairclips to stick in.

She knew that Mrs Tobin had plenty extra hairclips, she had seen a stand with dozens of packets of hairclips, as well as hairnets and brushes and bands, standing right at the front of the shop.

Beulah did not realise that Mrs Tobin was going to take her hair out of its braid. Maybe Mrs Tobin hadn't meant to either. It was such long, thick, magnificent hair, maybe Mrs Tobin couldn't help herself. Maybe that was why Joe had followed them into the back of the shop. He couldn't help himself either. Mrs Tobin's fingers worked gently through Beulah's hair, loosening it out, piece by piece. Mrs Tobin's touch was delicate. It felt so good, Beulah couldn't help herself either. It was wrong to let Mrs Tobin take down her hair. Louis had never seen her hair down, her own father hadn't seen her hair down. She should have got up and walked out. But the feel of Mrs Tobin's fingers was nicer than sugar. And even if she had the willpower to walk out, how could she have gone out into the main street of the town, her knee-length hair flying like a banner?

'Do you want a hand?' asked Joe, in a strained voice.

'Well, Joe, are you still here?' Mrs Tobin's voice was dreamy, as she worked her way to the bottom of the enormous braid and spread out the hair. It rippled over Beulah's black coat and spilled over at the sides onto the leatherette sofa.

'You can make yourself useful, so!' Mrs Tobin said, looking at Beulah's hair with satisfaction.

'You, I mean, young Dr Costello, go out there to the front of the shop where the toiletries are and get me a new hairbrush.'

Beulah blushed when Mrs Tobin said the word *toiletries*. It sounded like a bad word. Bertie had warned her that the infidels used lots of bad words. Naturally he hadn't told her what the bad words were, so she was always afraid an infidel would spring one upon her without her knowing.

Joe stood like a statue and didn't move.

125

'Will you get on and get it now,' said Mrs Tobin.

'What if I'm seen?' asked Joe, his face gone pink and luminous, even the whites of his eyes were pink around the edges.

'Oh for the love of God, let me out, myself,' said Mrs Tobin; she had to give a bit of a heave to manoeuvre her large body out of the seat. She clicked out noisily and Beulah stared after her because she didn't want to look at Joe. She tried to shake her hair behind her by shrugging her shoulders but it flowed around even more. Like a liquid drug. Deadly nightshade or maybe laudanum.

'Are you well?' Joe asked and then she had to look at him.

'We're all very healthy,' she said. 'We don't need doctors at all. Louis has a raw egg every morning,' she finished, proudly, even though she hated the way Louis drank down the raw egg with his Adam's apple bobbing and she dreaded the day she would see some stuck to his beard.

'I know you don't need doctors,' Joe said, very sadly. '*I* would never want to interfere with your religious views. I have the greatest respect for them. I hear that you are married now to Louis Kingston. I hope that it is all going well for the two of ye.'

'It is, it is, very well thank you.' Beulah sat in the middle of her hair, as mournful as a siren floating on a black sea. Joe put his hands in his pockets and began to whistle lightly, then stopped when he remembered that Poleites weren't allowed to listen to music. He walked up to the fireplace and began to tap the toe of his polished riding boot against the brass firearms. Mrs Tobin came bustling with a wooden-handled hairbrush with lemon-coloured bristles.

'Ah now, here is one that might do! I had my work cut out for me trying to find one strong enough.'

She sat down beside Beulah and brushed her hair gently. Beulah was surprised that Mrs Tobin didn't tell Joe to go away.

126

But Mrs Tobin was as mesmerised as Beulah herself, she hummed and muttered a little jaunty song to herself,

Let him go, let him tarry, let him sink or let him swim.
He doesn't care for me and I don't care for him.
He can go and find another whom I hope he will enjoy,
For I'm going to marry a far nicer boy.

Han Kingston had told Beulah that Poleites weren't strictly against music or singing, it was gramophones and radios that were the problem. Singing wasn't wrong just that Poleites were wary of what it might lead to. Not only was it associated with radios and gramophones, it was also associated with drinking, it might even lead to dancing.

Beulah hung on to that knowledge now. The knowledge that singing was not wrong. Electricity flowed up her neck and down her arms, she watched the flames on the coals. She'd never seen such colours, orange and pink and crimson at the front, blue and purple, like ghosts, behind.

When Mrs Tobin repeated the chorus a third time, Beulah wondered about Louis. Was Mrs Tobin referring to Louis and Beulah? But Louis did care about her and she wanted Mrs Tobin and Joe to know that.

'Louis is waiting for me,' she said. 'I'd better go.'

'Hold it a second,' said Mrs Tobin, she spoke lightly but there was a slight panic at the back of her voice. Joe cast Beulah a reproachful look.

'He'll get drenched,' Beulah said, jumping away from Mrs Tobin and her hairbrush.

'How?' asked Joe, looking out the window. 'There's no rain.'

'But wasn't there a heavy shower just now?' asked Beulah, sure that she'd been listening to the heavy beat of raindrops on the roof while Mrs Tobin was singing.

'There's been no rain at all,' said Mrs Tobin but she didn't look at Beulah as if she was mad. She acted as if it was usual to be wrong about these kind of things.

'Hand me the hairclips,' Mrs Tobin said to Joe. 'The poor girl is getting anxious. We shouldn't have kept her so long. He won't be cross with you, will he?'

Beulah didn't know what Mrs Tobin might think of Louis. She burned with loyalty. 'Louis would never say one word, he's like . . .' Beulah searched frantically and ended lamely, '. . . the Lamb of God.'

'Oh!' said Mrs Tobin, putting her hand on her heart. 'What a beautiful thing to say. Pass me those hairclips, Joe.'

Joe's face was serious. He said to Beulah, 'Are you not afraid of dying from the want of medicine?'

'I am afraid of nothing,' said Beulah. 'I'm very intrepid,' she added, remembering what the Reverend Moylan called her all those years ago.

'The beautiful words you have,' said Mrs Tobin. 'Are you a reader at all?'

'I read the Bible,' said Beulah, thinking of Bathsheba and how King David had seen her bathing. King David must have seen Bathsheba with her hair down. Han had told her often enough about the danger of hair, how it led to sin and slaughter.

'Such a good, good girl, you are,' said Mrs Tobin. 'Isn't she Joe?'

Joe nodded as he passed the hairclips. There was a sweet smell when he came near. It was wine, but Beulah didn't know what it was. It reminded her of the smell in Dr Costello's car, years before.

'Now, have you ever read Annie Smithson?' asked Mrs Tobin. 'She has the most beautiful stories. Canon Sheehan is another great writer. You might not want to read him, of course, he being of the wrong colour. Not that he isn't broad-minded, especially for a canon. But Annie Smithson now, she was born the same as yourself. Then she became a convert but you wouldn't mind that now would you?'

At first Beulah was puzzled, thinking that Mrs Tobin was saying that Annie Smithson was born a Poleite and Poleites didn't write novels or anything like novels. They read some novels. It was a bit hazy what was and wasn't allowed. *Frankenstein* was a good lesson to all, the Reverend Moylan said. But he didn't recommend it for the young. Bertie wasn't ready for it and Han said she didn't have the time and anyway she didn't need lessons. 'I couldn't agree, more,' answered the Reverend Moylan, admiringly, as usual. *Silas Marner*, that was the one for Beulah and Hester, he said. Beulah hated it. The old miser was boring and there were no such angelic children in real life. But the ideas about innocence and goodness and golden curls replacing gold coins was just what the Reverend Moylan liked. Beulah and Hester had to be so careful about what they were seen to be reading, that the idea of a Poleite actually writing something as frivolous as a novel was laughable.

But then, Beulah realised that Mrs Tobin was lumping her, Beulah, in with all other Protestants. Normally she would have been annoyed. Poleites hated this kind of ignorance, Bertie still seethed every time he remembered the man who took him for a Primitive Methodist, twenty years before. But somehow Beulah didn't really mind Mrs Tobin. Mrs Tobin did not seem prejudiced, Mrs Tobin was beguiling.

'*The Walk of a Queen*, now that's a lovely book. Is that the one about the time of the Troubles? You wouldn't want to read that or maybe you wouldn't mind.'

Beulah was not interested in reading Annie Smithson, she wasn't even thinking about Annie Smithson. She was thinking about how long she had been gone from Louis and how he might be worried or even cross. 'I don't mind,' she said to Mrs Tobin. 'But I must leave or else Louis will be fearful for me.'

'Look down there beside you,' said Mrs Tobin, who was still wrestling with Beulah's hair trying to get it into a bun. 'It has a blue cover.'

Beulah looked beside her on the sofa and where her hair had been just recently lying was a dark-blue-covered book.

'I don't know what one that is, but every single one of her books is better than the next. Take that off with you and there's no rush to return it.'

Beulah stuffed it into the pocket of her coat, glad for once that Han had made the pockets so big. She thanked Mrs Tobin and nodded shyly at Joe. She was full of confusion and her hair felt strange although very secure. She found it hard to walk. She was filled with wistful longing as Joe walked her out to the front door. When could she see him again to find out the medical names for the parts of the body? She couldn't live without them now after thinking about them for so long. Mysterious Latin words that resounded. No wonder the Catholics liked their Mass, with the Latin words running all through it, bouncing off their majestic ceilings.

Halfway across the wooden shop floor, Beulah stopped him. 'I can't be seen here with you, now. I wanted to know more about the names for bones, do you remember you told me before about the wrist and the ankle?'

Joe's face lit up, he took a step nearer, brushed her cheekbone with his soft white fingers. 'That's your Zygomatic arch.'

Beulah put her own hand up to her cheekbone, 'What do you call these purple marks under my eye.'

Joe scrutinised her face, Beulah had large violet-coloured smudges under her eyes. 'Well, they are not bones of course, you know,' he touched the hard ridge of bone underneath her left eye. 'That is your lower orbital margin.'

'I saw them when I was polishing the saucepans,' Beulah rubbed at the purple shadows again.

'Are you sleeping properly?' Joe asked.

'It is always hard to sleep,' Beulah said.

'I could write out a prescription for you, now,' Joe said.

Beulah gave him a frightened look, 'It is against my religion, don't you know that?'

'No one need ever know.' Joe took a step closer. 'Mrs Tobin wouldn't tell a soul.'

'No, no.' Beulah put her hand up in fright. 'I am not allowed medicine. I go for a walk every night, that's what helps me sleep afterwards. I stand by the mill and listen to the water.'

Joe looked interested, 'I have never seen the water-wheel working. My father told me about it when I was a boy. He saw it when he was a young fellow.'

'You could come to look at ours,' Beulah said, even though she knew that Joe could not come to look at the water-wheel while Louis was there.

Joe said, 'Louis wouldn't want strangers wandering around his place.'

'You're not a stranger,' Beulah said.

Joe didn't answer, he shook her hand solemnly before Beulah left the shop.

Chapter Thirteen

Louis's smooth cheeks were damp as if he'd been crying, his hat was pulled down over his eyes. Beulah could barely see the tip of his nose, his soft lips. She tried to talk to what she could see of him.

'I got talking to Mrs Tobin,' she tried out, unsurely. From the distance Louis's stiff-shouldered black figure looked angry. Now, she wasn't so sure.

'They say she is a nice woman,' Louis muttered, as he turned the trap for home.

Beulah thought that Louis was driving the pony too fast. The town streaked past her and she was afraid that he would use the whip too hard. They were soon on the outskirts of the town and into the countryside. The hawthorn hedges scraped across her view. They passed a few other pony and traps and several men with donkeys and carts but Louis did not say hello to them in his usual neighbourly fashion, only crouched in the front seat, driving like a devil.

Beulah gripped the seat tightly and hoped they would not meet Bertie or Han or the Reverend Moylan. Just as they were turning in their avenue she saw Danny Fox standing in the middle of the road with his mouth open. 'Good day, Louis,' he roared.

'Good day, Danny Fox,' said Louis and turned Sally quickly down the tree-lined drive.

They clattered into the cobbled yard and only then did Louis push up his hat so that she could see his face. She had never known Louis to get angry.

'Look at your hair, Beulah!' he shouted and turned to unharness Sally. He walked with Sally over to the stable and left Beulah standing there uncertainly, Shep fussing around the bottom of her long skirt. How could she look at her hair? They had no mirrors. Was there something in it to show that Joe had touched it? But, Joe hadn't touched her hair, she remembered, as she put her hand up to her cheekbone. How could Louis notice something like that?

She put her hand up to the front of her hair. It felt different, smoother, sweeping grandly over one ear from one side to the other. Beulah, like all the other Poleite women, usually had a flat centre parting and her hair was pulled back severely. She was still not sure what it looked like, but she could feel with her fingertips that it was glamorous. It felt like what the hairstyles of the women in the pictures in Mrs Tobin's shop might feel like.

How could Mrs Tobin have done it to her! Surely she must have known that a Poleite woman was not allowed to be fashionable or elegant. She could have met Han or Bertie or even the Reverend Moylan. They would have called a special meeting like they did that time that Sam Potts wouldn't stay away from the waitress in Bandon.

Louis was taking a long time and Beulah decided to walk into the house herself. She heaved the big shopping bag out of the cart and struggled to carry it in. She could hear Louis coming behind her now. He usually carried all the heavy bags. Before this, Beulah had thought that she didn't care whether Louis helped or not.

From the scullery, she could hear Louis clattering. She guessed that he was feeding Shep, so she crept back into the pantry and pulled out the book. Tucking it under her arm she ran down the dark passage.

133

Beulah looked down at the little blue volume in her hand. She hadn't even wanted it, she thought again angrily. Now she would have to hide it.

She could hear Louis in the kitchen room now, stoking the range. Shep was *her* dog who she'd brought from her own home and yet it was Louis who had remembered to feed her. Now he was doing the fire and he would probably make the tea as well. She should go in and help him but she couldn't because she had to get up to old Uncle Georgie's room to hide Mrs Tobin's book. She ran upstairs away from the sound of Louis's shovelling, the scream of the whistle from the old kettle. Pushing in the door quickly, she went to the half empty bookshelves. She placed the book between two other blue-bound books, hoping that it would pass for another of grand-uncle Georgie's books, although it seemed to Beulah that the title and author were screaming out from the spine in deadly black letters, *The Walk of a Queen* by Annie P. Smithson.

Converts. Bertie had told her about them and he said that they were always women. Brainwashed by the priests, drugged with incense and soft talk from nuns. Or Latin words, maybe? Beulah considered that possibility. However it was managed, Bertie said, they got tricked into becoming Catholics. They were always sorry afterwards when they ended up scrubbing floors in convents, making sandwiches for priests and embroidering the priests' vestments for the rest of their days.

'Couldn't they come back?' Beulah dared to ask once.

'And who would have them back after all that?' asked Bertie.

'Isn't it only kind and Christian to take them back?' asked Beulah surprised.

'I wouldn't take a girl like that back, no sirree. I wouldn't even if it was yourself.' Bertie caught Beulah's eye with a hard stare.

'Look here, child,' Bertie went on. 'You know I've nothing against my Catholic neighbours at all. I'm fond of every one of

134

them and I'm the first to run to them when they're in trouble. But girls who run out of families and cause trouble just to be bowing down in front of the same God in a different church don't deserve to be taken back.'

'Do you believe they've got the same God?' Beulah asked.

'Of course I do,' said Bertie. 'But he likes us better, you know.'

'Do you think so?' Beulah asked, thinking about the half a bag of sugar she had eaten in secret that very week.

'Aren't we doing all the right things, sure?' Bertie rasped his hand across his chin. 'I don't know what the Lord would do without the Poleites!'

Beulah touched the front of her hair again and began to take the pins out. She flattened it as hard as she could with her fingers, rapidly plaiting it into her usual style. Her fingers were sure and steady now that she was out of the town. She thought about Bertie, the whole time she was working on her hair.

Bertie didn't know anything about Beulah. He still called her child though she was touching six feet. Beulah thought about the hard stare that Bertie had given her. She never knew why it worried her. She was not about to run away to become a convert, she didn't care about God enough to make such an effort.

Louis was sitting by the table. He had made the tea in the blue and white striped pot, a cake box from the confectioner's stood beside the teapot. Beulah went over to the table and scraped out the wooden chair. 'Cake, when did you get the cake?' she asked.

Louis looked up at her, his eyes were huge and black in the dim kitchen, his pupils dilated to cover nearly all the blue iris.

'Aren't I the one who should be asking questions?' He poured the tea into her cup. Beulah stared at the tea in the white cup. It was very strong, he knew that she didn't like it strong.

135

'How do you mean?' she asked. She wanted to sound gentle, but her voice came out sour.

'I mean what I say and here's question for you now.' Beulah cringed under his new and hateful voice. 'Why did you say you wanted to go to Mrs Tobin's for castor oil when you had something else on your mind entirely?'

'But I did get the castor oil,' Beulah insisted, guiltily.

'I know you did, but what happened to your hair?'

'It fell down.'

'It fell down, did it now? Since when did a Poleite woman's hair fall down in public?'

'It didn't really fall down, it was going to, and anyway I've got away more hair than the other women. You know that.'

'I don't go around comparing women's hair, I've better things to do, so I have. You went to the hairdresser's didn't you?'

'I did not. I never went near Nora O'Neill's salon in my life. It's a filthy-looking place.'

Louis raised his voice slightly, 'You left me like a fool in the main street with every infidel in the town looking at me.'

Beulah swallowed and raised her voice, 'Can you not remember our wedding? Reverend Moylan told you that you were never to doubt me. That you were to cleave to me.'

'And what would the Reverend Moylan say about you? Leaving a fellow Poleite out there, exposed like that, surrounded by corner Johnnies.'

'And what could I do with my hair after falling down? Did you expect me to walk down the main street like a tramp?'

If Joe Costello hadn't been there what would have happened then? Mrs Tobin might have noticed her, but maybe she mightn't have noticed her if she hadn't heard Joe speaking. And maybe she *would* have walked out of the shop with her hair falling down. Beulah could feel the sensation of her hair slipping down from its clips, falling down over her neck. The whole of the town, the corner Johnnies, the town girls laughing at her.

136

'Why didn't you tell me my hair was falling down? Hunched like an old man on that trap, caring for nothing and nobody. I was in no hairdresser's, but if it wasn't for Joe Costello coming to my aid I'd be the laughing stock of the whole town.'

She could see then that he would have believed her now and that she shouldn't have mentioned Joe Costello.

'Joe Costello the doctor's son?'

'He's a doctor himself now.'

'How do you know?'

'He told me himself.'

Louis's face was still for a while, then he quietly asked her questions. She told him a version of what had gone on in Mrs Tobin's back room, carefully omitting any reference to *The Walk of a Queen* by Annie Smithson.

'So what exactly did he call you?'

'I think he called me Mrs Kingston.'

'How did he know you were married, I wonder?'

'*I* don't know, do I? Sure, maybe he said, *Miss* Kingston.'

'Maybe he did,' said Louis. 'Go on.'

'So he said, "Excuse me, madam, I mean Miss Kingston, I think your hair is going to fall down." '

'So he went away then with himself, I hope?'

'He did, yes.'

'And what kind of a woman is this Mrs Tobin? Is she a decent infidel?'

'Oh, very decent and kind and a welcome for everybody.'

'How do you know she has a welcome for everybody? Was there someone else there while she was fixing your hair?'

'Nobody.' Beulah couldn't meet his eye.

'There was someone else there, wasn't there?'

Louis stood up, 'Joe Costello was there, I'll wager.'

Beulah remained silent, she didn't know what else she could do.

Louis went and sat on the other chair again, he took his cup

137

up and washed the tea leaves around the side of his cup, like a tinker about to tell fortunes. His shoulders were stiff and straight, as if he'd a coat hanger inside his black coat.

'So you let an infidel, worse still a butchering doctor, see your hair when no one else not even your husband has seen it?'

'You're not allowed to see my hair anyway, so you're not.'

'I am so.'

'Who said so?'

'The Reverend Moylan said so. I was expecting to see it the night we got married. He said that I would see it. Only I thought that you were shy, I was giving you a chance.'

'You were the one who was shy,' Beulah persisted.

'Maybe I was, maybe I was,' Louis's colour was rising, 'but I thought that you were too. I was having respect for your feelings and that is the size of it.'

Beulah stood up too. She had her hand over where she thought her heart was, the lower border of her rib cage. She pressed hard against the bone, hurting herself as much as she could. If she hurt herself enough, maybe Louis would stop asking questions.

But Louis continued to look at her bitterly. Beulah took her hand down from her rib cage, she had always thought that it would be Louis who would do the placating. 'I am awful sorry,' she said. 'I mean that.'

'I am.' Beulah pulled the clips out of her hair. It fell over her face and she pushed it back. Louis looked at the floor.

'Look at my hair!' She pulled at his arm like a lonely child, but Louis would not look at her hair.

'I can't look at it, now,' he said, but he took her hand. 'Let us go on up to sleep.'

They went up the dark passage and as they passed Uncle Georgie's room, Beulah told Louis about *The Walk of a Queen*, trying to explain her helplessness. Throwing the blame, 'And I was telling her that I did not want it, but she kept on.'

138

Louis wanted to go and see Mrs Tobin, 'You shouldn't have let her order you like that. She will have to take that book back.'

'She meant well, she was only trying to be kind, I didn't want to have no manners.'

'She knew full well what she was doing. What interest does she think you could possibly have in what a convert has to say?'

Beulah shrugged inside her long white nightgown. Their bedroom was very warm, their heads drooping with tiredness. Outside a low whine started up.

'Is it Shep?' asked Louis.

Beulah sat up stiff, listening. 'It's not like her. But she must be growling at something.'

'I'd better go down,' said Louis, lowering his legs over the side of the bed.

'I'll come with you,' said Beulah.

'There is no need,' said Louis but he was glad when she insisted, tying her hair back and buttoning her long black overcoat over her nightgown. Louis stuffed his night shirt inside his big black trousers and they set off together, hurrying down the stairs to the back door.

Outside, the full moon hung over the old beech trees, Shep was straining her neck out from behind one of the trees and Beulah wondered why she wasn't running to meet her. She broke into a run, calling Shep's name out loud.

Shep lay behind the tree, trying to rise up from her hindquarters and failing. Licking Beulah's face and hands, whining as Beulah tried to examine her in the light of Louis's bicycle lamp.

'It is the right hind leg,' said Louis, holding it up and Beulah was glad for Shep that Louis's hands were dry and warm and gentle. 'How did it happen at all?'

It was clearly broken, limp and bloodied, hanging at an awkward angle.

139

'It's gone all right, it must have been a car,' said Louis.

'Whose car I wonder?' said Beulah. There was a silence then. Louis didn't answer and Beulah wished that she hadn't asked that question. Dr Costello's was one of the few cars around.

'Well,' said Louis. 'An accident is always better than an illness. A clean break heals in no time.'

Poleites preferred accidents to disease. Disease was mysterious and malignant, it came from the inside and it stank. Accidents came from outside and they were clean. Breaks and cuts. They could be bound up and splinted. They healed up quickly if they were kept clean. They could be the cleanest way to die, too. The sudden snap of the neck after a fall from a horse, a head split open on the road after a skid on the ice.

Beulah and Louis carried Shep gently into the kitchen and then Louis went out to the shed to look for a splint.

Shep lay, looking over her shoulder at Beulah, she had stopped whining, but her well-behaved silence was harder to bear. Out in the pantry, Beulah removed a white cloth from the can of milk on the pantry shelf. She took a mug from the hook overhead and scooped two mugfuls into the saucepan. She went to the cupboard and emptied a small heap of sugar into the milk. An old biscuit tin in the corner caught her attention for a moment.

'Shep,' she called out and Shep whined back. 'What about a nice bit of shop bread?' Shep whined again and Beulah ran into the kitchen with the tin under one arm and the saucepan in the other hand. 'Look what I've got here for my pet!' She opened the tin and took out a piece of L-shaped bread with a dark brown shiny crust. Once a week, the baker delivered cottage loaf to Old Mrs Sheehan. It was shaped like the back seat of a car and there were divisions along the length of it. Nellie broke off however much a customer needed. It was Beulah's favourite bread but she always had to have an excuse to buy it because Poleite women were expected to bake their own. Beulah had been hiding this piece for herself, now she wanted Shep to have it.

Beulah lit the gas and was slowly heating the milk and bread and sugar when Louis came in with a thin small slat of wood and a few old strips of linen.

'Let that alone for a while until I get the splint on her,' said Louis. 'Have you washed her paw?'

'I didn't think of that,' said Beulah, going over to the range to get the kettle. 'A small dropeen of disinfectant would be no harm,' Louis said and took a brown bottle with a cross on it from the bottom of the dresser. 'Bertie only ever uses salt,' said Beulah.

'Well, I use this the whole time,' said Louis. 'My biggest fear is gangrene.'

The brown liquid went down into the hot water in a milky cloud and a sharp, sweet clean smell rose up. 'Isn't it beautiful?' said Beulah.

'Oh, it's great altogether,' said Louis. 'You can put it in your bath and all.'

Shep let Beulah bathe her paw without a murmur. Beulah thought that there were tears in the dog's eyes until she realised it was her own eyes that were brimming with tears. Louis took out a blue handkerchief and wiped them. Beulah inclined her head and then together they wiped Shep's paw with a rough towel. Their heads touched for a moment and Beulah stepped back while Louis bound Shep's paw tightly against the slat.

Beulah went to heat up the goody, stirring it with a wooden spoon to dissolve the sugar. Louis stayed sitting beside Shep, stroking her head. 'I hope it works right now, I wouldn't like her to have a crooked leg,' he said.

'Have you done many of them?' Beulah was drowsy, the smell of the milk heating reminded her of Han, of home at bedtime and when she was ill.

'This is the first, now, that I've done for real,' said Louis.

'You looked like an expert to me.'

'Do you remember our old cat, Blackie?'

'The fat one, who never moved except to follow the sun around the yard all day, wasn't she Blackie?'

'That's her, that's the one, well I used to practise on her.'

'And did she mind?'

'Mind? She used to love it, she used to lie back as happy as a lamb with two mothers!' Louis smiled and for a moment, despite his straggly old beard, Beulah felt he was his boyhood self again.

The milk nearly boiled over.

Louis got an old china soup plate from the dresser, white with a midnight-blue rim touched with gold.

'Use that,' said Louis. 'T'will cool quicker in that.'

'Are you sure?' asked Beulah. 'Weren't these your mother's good ones?'

'And it isn't as if Shep is going to break it now, is it?' said Louis, pointing to Shep, who was lying like a statue except when Beulah touched her and her tail moved.

'Get her onto that old couch, now.'

Beulah took the head, murmuring to Shep that everything was all right now, while Louis supported the back and hindquarters. The couch was an old leatherette one, sunk down into itself beside the Stanley range. It was the leatherette that reminded Beulah of Mrs Tobin and Joe Costello. She looked at Louis.

'Are you all right?' asked Louis.

'Grand,' said Beulah, not wanting to look at him. He would never have suede gaiters or a smooth chin. He had no Latin words. It was too bad.

Louis thought that she was hungry, he insisted on making more goody. Shep had finished hers when Beulah and Louis sat on either side of Shep, their heads bent over the steaming bowls.

'Why don't you have some sugar?' Louis brought over the

142

rosy china bowl and a spoon and held them in front of Beulah. 'I think you need more sugar than a normal person on account of being so tall, like.'

'No.' Beulah didn't want his kindness now. She didn't want him making up excuses for her so that she could eat sugar. 'I should not be eating it, I know I shouldn't.'

'I'm not going to tell Reverend Moylan,' said Louis, wrinkling his forehead at her.

'Do you not believe in him then?' asked Beulah, hopefully. She thought that maybe if they didn't believe, they could run away. Louis didn't answer at first.

'Do you not believe in the Poleite religion?' Beulah questioned again eagerly.

'I believe all right, but I think you need sugar . . . sometimes people need things. Doesn't the Reverend have to take honey now or he faints?'

'But do you believe in Poleites?' persisted Beulah.

'Of course I do,' said Louis, disappointingly. 'I was brought up to it.'

'And is that enough of a reason?' Beulah asked.

Louis put up his hand, to stop her from saying anymore. 'It is a good reason because, number one, I'm a natural Christian, and number two, the Poleites are the best Christians I know, and if anyone of us now was to strike off on our own, how would we manage without the Reverend? How would we know the difference between right or wrong or what do when we were sick?'

Shep sighed and moved her head onto Louis's lap. Beulah stared at Shep for a moment before jealously patting Shep's rough head until Shep put her head back on Beulah's lap. She rested her hand lightly on Shep's head. Louis scratched gently along the line of Shep's spine while Shep gave out deep sighs and gazed lovingly at Louis. Beulah jealously rubbed Shep's head again and bent over her, murmuring endearments, blocking Shep's view of Louis.

Louis rustled around and came over with a bag of white sugar and a spoon. 'Go on,' he said. 'It's good when you have a shock.'

'What shock did I have?'

'Shep's accident,' he said, looking at her with surprise.

'Oh, Shep,' said Beulah, turning away from the spoon that Louis was holding out.

'And everything else as well, today was a hard day for you.' Louis stood there as Beulah cast her mind back over the day. Joe and Mrs Tobin, *The Walk of a Queen*.

'Do you think she was trying to convert you?' Louis asked.

'Who?' asked Beulah, trying to pretend that Louis wasn't reading her thoughts.

Louis cleared his throat, but he still sounded hoarse when he said all the things she had been fearing he would say, even though she didn't know that she was fearing those things until he said them.

Louis struck his stomach, it seemed to be where he thought his heart was. 'Since the day I first saw you. You came down the lane with your father and you had those long jet black plaits and you must have been only four and a half and I always wanted to hold your hair and see what it looked like spread out around you. Even when I was that young, I wanted to see it taken out.' Louis stopped for a moment and it was clear that he was thinking how it was Joe Costello who had seen it first. Beulah couldn't bear to hear him saying it again.

'I'll have the sugar, so,' she said.

She thought of her mother and Reverend Moylan and how he'd opened his mouth to her mother like a baby bird that day he fainted. Louis handed her the brown paper bag and the spoon and went on. 'One day, you know, down by the river you called me brother, but I knew that I was going to marry you.' He cleared his throat again. 'Eat up anyway. If you don't give yourself the things that you need, you can get desperate sick. My mother was always denying and fasting. And the true

144

Poleites don't really like it, you know. Aren't the Catholics always at it, instead of getting on with their work. It's only a form of indulgence.'

The clock struck the hour. It was ten o'clock, an unearthly time for any Poleite to be up and about. They never stayed up late. In summer they went to bed when the light went; in the winter they used Aladdin lamps and went to bed at nine to save the oil.

'Will we get Shep a blanket?' asked Louis.

'No, she will be lonely,' said Beulah, her eyes wide open and sparkling from all the sugar. 'Can't we bring her with us?' Beulah was sure that Louis would refuse.

'All right so,' he said, and they lifted Shep up the stairs and down the dark passages, and when they got into the warm tucked-away bedroom, Shep looked as if she was going to take fright. Louis and Beulah took off their overcoats and lay on either side of Shep, talking to her. Beulah had always wanted to keep Shep in the bed with her when she was a child, but she wouldn't have been allowed. She patted Shep, gently, 'That's the good girl now.'

Louis talked to Shep, too. 'Who's the brainy girl?'

Shep closed her eyes and went off. Beulah knew that Louis was waiting for her to speak first so she went silent and shut her eyes. She thought that Louis might ask her if she was asleep but after a while Louis fell asleep himself and then she was sorry.

Shep's damp nose got dry and hot. Beulah fretted. Maybe the room was too hot for a dog. Maybe they would roll over and squash her in their sleep. Louis was dreaming. Once he sat up straight and shouted out from the Book of Kings, 'I've got my hook through your nose and my bridle between your lips and I'll lead thee back the way thou camest.'

Shep began to dream. Twitching and trembling. Waving her paws in the air.

Beulah thought about Joe Costello's brown suede gaiters. As

145

children, Beulah and Hester had been told about the emptiness of outward show. Beulah had been proud of her own lack of vanity. She had never cared what she wore. Now, Joe Costello had changed everything, telling her that he liked her because she was natural. She had been far too pleased about her wedding dress. It must have been vanity allowed her to let Mrs Tobin take down her hair for Joe Costello's admiration. *The Walk of a Queen* was still sitting on Uncle Georgie's shelves. She had to burn that book.

She lowered her legs over the side of the bed, wondering if it was midnight. Han had always said that it was very unhealthy to stay up past half past nine in the evening.

As Beulah turned the handle of Georgie's bedroom door and approached the shelf, a cockroach scurried across the floor. She screamed. Not loudly, but enough to wake Louis, she thought. She wanted him to come down and help her to burn *The Walk of a Queen* and talk about Uncle Georgie.

You could go mad from lack of sleep. Bertie knew a Poleite who stayed up a whole night once to save the hay. By morning time, he was raving. He even forgot that he was a Poleite and he was carted off to a mental hospital. The minister had to go and rescue him. 'And didn't he manage to calm him down, by Jove! You see a lot of this mental carry-on is only all in the mind. Like the hypochondriacs, a man wakes up, thinks he's gone mad and then he says to himself, I better act mad and catches the hysterics.'

Beulah took down a couple of books of poetry and flicked through them. The pages were gilt-edged and thin, they rustled between her fingers. She wished she understood this kind of poetry. They had learned some in school, simple verse that stayed in her mind even though Bertie warned her to have no truck with such stuff. 'Nearly as bad as the Hail Mary!' Bertie exclaimed.

Stretching out her hand, Beulah took out the dark blue cloth-bound book. She opened the title page: *The Walk of a Queen* by Annie P. Smithson. A vein pounded somewhere in her head and a fluttering went through the blood of her legs. If she had become a convert, she could have married Joe Costello.

Upstairs, there was a click. Beulah heard footsteps. She boldly held *The Walk of a Queen* up against her chest in an obvious way just in case Louis might think that she was trying to hide it. Flinging open the door with her left hand, she marched out of Georgie's room with her head held high in the air.

Louis stopped halfway down the stairs, 'Shh, you'll wake Shep again.'

'Was she awake?' Beulah asked anxiously.

'She woke me whimpering, I think that she was looking for you.'

'And is she awake now?' Beulah asked.

'I got her back to sleep myself, patting her and talking to her.'

Beulah gave him a jealous look. She was always afraid that Shep might begin to love Louis more than she loved Beulah. 'Will you come down with me to the Stanley, I am going to burn this book tonight.'

147

Chapter Fourteen

The X-ray room was full of whirring ticking noises. Beyond there was a rushing sound that reminded Beulah of the river and the day Louis took herself and Hester down through Stanley's field. She heard Hester's little rustling whispers to Mrs Treadle behind the control panel, like an undercurrent to the big river X-ray noises.

'Dr Kumar is on his way,' said Nurse Bolton in an authoritative voice. There was a stir of excitement behind the control panel and Beulah worried about Hester. Hester had never seen an Indian before. Could she be trusted not to gasp or stare? Beulah kept her eyes closed. Let them think what they liked.

There was a click of heels and a cloud of scent descended over Beulah's face. She opened her eyes immediately. Dr Kumar was even more vivid then she remembered him. His well-trimmed beard shining, blue black. Nothing like a Poleite beard. 'I see you have returned to us, Mrs Kingston,' he said, his sing-song voice reminding Beulah of a Welsh labourer who had worked on Fox's farm one summer, years ago.

Mrs Treadle ran out, carrying a sky-blue apron. She stood on tiptoe, her small feet threatening to slip out of her black high-heeled shiny mules, and Dr Kumar struggled to put the sky-blue rubbery thing over his head. It was shaped like a painting apron that Beccy had as a child.

Beccy's was scarlet, with grey elephants. When Beccy was three, she stayed for a weekend at Hollywood House and Hester and Beulah sent her out to the garden to paint. The sight of the paintbox and brushes filled them with fright, they hadn't had such things when they were children. What if Beccy splashed the paint around? Even in the garden, Hester worried about Beccy splashing the flowers. But Hester always fussed. Even now, Beulah could hear her whispering anxiously to Mrs Treadle.

'What is that for?' Beulah pointed at Dr Kumar's sky-blue rubber-plated chest.

'Radiation protection,' sang Dr Kumar cheerfully as he went down to the end of the trolley and took hold of Beulah's tough-skinned hands. His hands were as soft as butter.

'How come you get one and I don't?' asked Beulah, ignoring the frown that Hester was directing at her from behind the control panel. Beulah's fists were clenched tight with fear. She thought of the Reverend Moylan and his stories about people exposed to radiation who were doomed to go around for years with growths and tumours hanging off them like apples and pears. Before they died terrible roaring deaths, cut off from the comfort of the one true God.

Dr Kumar's eyes were kind but distant, he looked beyond Beulah as if there were wide open spaces behind her.

'Mrs Treadle is better able to explain all that to you, now.' He gripped her hand, tightly.

But Mrs Treadle was busy too, propping a steel X-ray plate by the side of Beulah's head with a big plastic bottle full of liquid. 'Ah now, Beulah, it is very technical and I can't be holding up Dr Kumar because he is wanted in theatre as we speak. You must trust us, don't you know that you're as safe as anything.'

Beulah looked over at Hester, whose small white fluffy head was nodding away to every word Mrs Treadle uttered.

'But why can't I have one too?'

'Now, Beulah how would we get it over your shoulders and anyway, the doctor has to have one because he has to work with radiation all the time.'

'But, then it isn't safe.'

'Beulah, you're only getting a teeny-tiny point o eight of a second, it is nothing and Dr Kumar is getting your scattered radiation which is more dangerous.'

Beulah couldn't let the matter drop. She wanted to, she could see Dr Kumar looking impatient. 'But what if it scatters back off him on top of me.'

'Ah, now, Beulah, stop. Don't be asking me to get technical with you. We'll get no work done and the waiting room is chock-a-block.'

Dr Kumar stood up and said, 'Get another apron for her, or we'll be here all night!'

'Well, there is really no need at all,' said Mrs Treadle and she went out of the room, her heels clicking like tiny hammers.

Beulah avoided Hester's eyes and Dr Kumar looked into his wide open spaces. Mrs Treadle came back with another apron, a white one this time, covered with large orange sunflowers. Beulah's body jerked with the weight of it as Mrs Treadle slapped it down not very gently. But she was a lot more gentle than she wanted to be, Beulah guessed from the look on her face.

'Right, are we ready now?' asked Dr Kumar, drawing himself back with a great effort from his wide open spaces. Beulah lay under the apron. It was heavy like the soil that would lie over her body one day. She hoped she would get to the grave sooner rather than later, before she had the time to develop those tumours that Reverend Moylan talked about.

Mrs Treadle made grinding noises with some switch behind the control panel and then she ran out and put her hand on Beulah's arm.

'You are really fine, you know. Look, I'm only giving point o eight of a second and with the apron now there's no fear of you at all.' Beulah could see that Mrs Treadle regretted the slapping-down of the apron. Dr Kumar joined in with general forgiveness, too giving her hands a well-meaning squeeze. Beulah opened her eyes and Hester waved.

Mrs Treadle ran back behind the control panel and made a few more grinding sounds. 'Ready now?' shouted Dr Kumar.

'Prepping and EXPOSE!' roared Mrs Treadle to the accompaniment of a great rushing clicking noise from the X-ray tube pointed at Beulah's neck. As Mrs Treadle shouted 'expose!', Dr Kumar pulled down on Beulah's arms with such force she thought they would be sucked out of their sockets.

'Great,' said Mrs Treadle running out after a few seconds when the light had gone off in the X-ray camera. There was a still a rushing noise from the X-ray tube but Mrs Treadle didn't notice it. Maybe it was dangerous, radiation still leaking out, splattering or scattering on top of them all.

'You can come out now,' Mrs Treadle said to Hester. 'I'm going to the darkroom with this. I hope you gave them a good pull,' she said Dr Kumar. 'We don't want to be repeating Mrs Kingston when she's so nervous of the radiation.'

'Anyway,' Mrs Treadle went on busily, without giving Dr Kumar a chance to reply, 'Beulah's got a nice long neck. We should have the seven of them.'

'The seven what?' said Beulah.

'Seven cervical vertebrae,' said Dr Kumar. 'Your neck is also known as the cervical spine and it is made up of seven little bones.'

'They're all joined together,' went on Dr Kumar. 'And they all have a little hole and the spinal cord goes up through them all taking messages to your brain.'

'Isn't that very interesting,' said Hester and Beulah closed her eyes wearily. She would have liked Dr Kumar to herself for a minute. How could she find it interesting now if Hester was getting excited about it as well?

Mrs Treadle came running back in with a black and white film in her hand. 'What a beautiful picture, even if I say so myself!' Mrs Treadle clipped it onto the front of a white box on the wall and pressed a switch, a light flickered a couple of times inside the box and then illuminated the side of a skull with a grinning mouth and a long long neck skeleton made up of a row of bony knobs.

'Very pretty picture, Mrs Treadle. You can see right down almost as far as T2,' said Dr Kumar, moving close to the picture, putting his right hand around his chin as he looked into the shadows.

Mrs Treadle looked very happy. Hester stood beside her, smiling. But Hester didn't know the first thing about good or bad X-ray pictures so what was she laughing about?

'Are ye going to stand around all night praising yourselves?' said Beulah.

'Indeed you are right,' said Dr Kumar. 'I must get back to the theatre!'

'There's crowds outside,' said Mrs Treadle.

'But am I dead or alive or what?' asked Beulah.

Dr Kumar turned around. 'Apart from a bit of wear and tear which is quite normal at your age, you're absolutely right as rain.'

'Wear and tear!' shouted Beulah. 'What's that?' But there was nothing left of Dr Kumar apart from his lingering perfume. Mrs Treadle was already wheeling her trolley towards the door.

'I'm finished! Aren't I?'

'Now, now, now,' said Mrs Treadle.

'Don't now, now me. Haven't I seen my own death's head grinning at me and ye all stood around laughing, including my own sister.'

'Beulah!' said Hester.

'Oh I don't care if I'm finished or not. It's just one would think that people would have the politeness to tell one after one went to the trouble of coming in for the X-ray.'

'She never got over the death of her son, John,' whispered Hester to Mrs Treadle. 'It broke her heart.'

It disgusted Beulah the way Hester could come out and talk to strangers like that just because she admired them. Anyway Hester was wrong. It wasn't John that broke her heart.

John had always looked like Louis. Even as a child he had those red marks on his knees that Louis had. Always kneeling. In all the same places, on the cobbles, on the grass beside the puppies. Kneeling for hours by the stone trough, pouring water from one vessel to another. He was a good boy, thoughtful of Leah. It wasn't that Leah wasn't thoughtful, too. It was just that John had a way about him that was *too* kind, that reminded her of Louis.

There hadn't been any dogs for a long time at Hollywood House. Not since Louis had shot Shep. For years Leah and John had begged for a dog. Now and then Hester took up their case, 'Children need pets.'

'They're too much trouble,' Beulah said.

'But especially for Poleites,' Hester went on.

'Why Poleites?' asked Beulah.

'Because of the loneliness of course,' said Hester. 'Of course you don't remember what it was like to not have a pet. You always had Shep by your side.'

Beulah stopped to look at Hester. The words sounded pettish but Hester's face wasn't. Her blue eyes were wide open and enquiring.

'I hate to think of children being lonely,' Hester said.

Beulah was sad that she couldn't please her.

'I was lonely too,' said Beulah. 'School especially. If you hadn't been with me I don't know what I'd have done.'

153

'There you are!' said Hester. 'That was because you didn't have Shep at school.'

Louis walked up the yard holding the gun awkwardly, as if he wasn't a farmer at all. He held it like a city man or a young boy who had never seen a gun in his life.

'Can you not hear me, am I talking to myself? I said no and that is final.'

Beulah rarely raised her voice and on this occasion it was hardly a shout. She wanted to give Hester a fright so that Hester would leave her alone.

Hester continued on as if nothing unusual had occurred, 'Isn't it queer to have a farmhouse without a dog too?'

'Are you deaf or what?'

John wasn't. He came running into the room with his blue eyes bulging. 'Mama, mama. Are oo hurt?'

'Are *you* hurt?' Beulah corrected him.

'Are oo?' John persisted. He was seven and spoke well except when he was excited or anxious. He threw himself up against her apron, gasping. The front of his shirt was wet and his knees were bright red with prickly marks.

'Hester is trying to get me to get you a dog,' said Beulah and then went on boldly in spite of the look on Hester's face. 'But it would upset Mama a lot you know.'

Beulah took hold of John's hand. 'All dogs die and when they die they break your heart. I had a dog called Shep and I haven't been the same since she died.'

John peered into Beulah's face. She hardly ever explained anything. He put out his hand and touched her cheek, it tickled the nerves on the side of her face. She tried to wipe the red prickly marks from his knee but the marks continued to stand out angrily. Beulah gave a dismissive nod at Hester over his shoulder and Hester walked away giving Beulah reproachful

154

looks. 'So you must never ask for a dog again, John. You wouldn't like to upset Mama, would you?' John shook his head. 'Now, how about a spoon of sugar?' asked Beulah but John shook his head. He said that he wasn't hungry, that Leah was waiting for him. He ran off and Beulah knew that he wouldn't mention it again. She knew that she would hear no more about a dog from Leah either. John would make sure of that.

Furtively, from the upstairs windows, she watched John playing around the farm with Leah. Sometimes Hester ran out in her granny-print apron and had a chase around the yard with Leah and John. And the sight of Hester, acting so young, made Beulah's eyes fill up with tears. Beulah felt that she deserved to be excluded. Beulah felt old and she looked old. She was twenty-five and gaunt. She longed for her hair to go grey so that she could be completely finished with any idea of youth.

John and Leah and Hester played and Beulah watched, and at the end of two months, Beulah decided that the children were not lonely. That they were happy. Hester had been dwelling on her own unhappy youth, not really thinking about John and Leah.

Beulah's own childhood had been unhappy. Shep hadn't kept away the loneliness. It had nothing to do with having dogs or not. It had to do with being a Poleite. Some days at school no one looked at her, not even the teacher. Sometimes, for instance during the Angelus, everyone stared at her. She often went into the little woods on their farm after school and cried. It seemed a luxury now to have the spare time for crying. After she left school, she never had the time for tears again.

While Beulah and Hester were at school they were given plenty of free time for homework and also what Bertie called 'growing time for the brain'. But once Beulah left school she was expected to work hard in the house. She had always liked

155

cleaning, it gave her privacy but now Han was training her to cook and bake. Beulah hated cooking, it messed up the place and besides, she was being prepared for marriage and she didn't like it.

Three months before she left school Han remarked to Bertie one evening that Beulah had had enough *growing time* for her brain and brought down an old copybook covered in brown paper and began to read recipes at Beulah.

Beulah hated the sore redness in the palms of her hands from beating sugar and butter together. 'You can't have it creamy enough for a nice cake, put in plenty of elbow grease!' Han thundered in the kitchen. Hester wasn't being pressured in the same way at all and Beulah couldn't understand it. Why was Hester being allowed to sit for hours on end, indulging herself? Herself and her prim lips, her embroidery designs, her quilted sewing box.

If Beulah decided to go for a walk herself, she couldn't get as far as the start of the woods, without Han roaring something about pickles or pastry or lemon curd.

Beulah had to run faster and faster every evening on her walk, Han allowing her less and less time. Soon Han could be heard roaring before she'd even started. 'Apple tart now, Beulah, come on!'

The last month at school was June. They walked along the hot roads and picked whortleberries and wild flowers for Han even though she kept telling them that they were too old now to be bringing her things home in jam pots.

There were worse things than loneliness, Beulah thought as she went from window to window, peering at Hester and the two children. John didn't seem to care about dogs anymore. He ignored all the dogs he met now. On the road or in the town. Leah still patted them but John looked into the distance. Even though it was John that they followed. John moved away from

156

dogs, crossed to the other side of the road or the street for even the town dogs seemed to be fond of him.

'He's sick of dogs, they won't leave him alone,' Beulah said.

'No, they won't leave him alone, will they?' said Hester.

Danny Fox's sheepdog followed John for a half mile one day, sniffing at his heels and whining. Afterwards, of course, Beulah knew that she should have allowed John his dog.

PART THREE

Chapter Fifteen

Four weeks later, Beulah was back for more X-rays. This time the arthritis could be seen clearly. Even Beulah could see the raggedy look on the bones of her neck. Why wasn't it clear before, Beccy wanted to know. They admitted it was worse, that they had never seen it to spread so fast. Dr Kumar shook his head, Mrs Treadle put her hand sympathetically on Beulah's arm.

'Nothing had shown up then,' Mrs Treadle said. 'God, has no one anything better to do than criticise doctors? Dr Kumar is half dead from lack of sleep.'

There were no more sprightly people talking about medical miracles. The waiting room was full of sad people and it smelt of wet dogs. The rain drummed on the window panes. The outside door kept opening and closing, letting in cold draughts. It was clear that Mrs Treadle had far too much work to do. She said so herself.

'Excuse me, sorry now, that I don't know your name,' Mrs Treadle addressed Beccy. 'But I haven't time to sit around discussing things. And I'm not qualified, either.' Mrs Treadle turned her back on them and began busily shepherding an old man out of one of the changing cubicles.

Beulah sat in a flimsy wheelchair. SOUTHERN HEALTH BOARD was stencilled across the back of the wheelchair in great white letters, it swayed dangerously every time Beulah moved and the brakes didn't work. Beulah got out of the wheelchair and limped over to a bench to wait for the ambulance. She said that she felt better and the pain had subsided. When they arrived home, Beulah put the kettle on and made tea for them all. But she did not stay mobile for long, the pain came back even fiercer.

Two weeks into December, Leah rang and said that she wasn't coming home for Christmas, Hester took the call. The way Hester handled the call, caused arguments right through the Christmas holidays and beyond. 'It would be *you* who was standing next to it when it rang!' Beulah said, time after time.

Beccy was in the hall, getting Beulah ready to take her out for a drive in the wheelchair. Beulah and Beccy fixed their eyes urgently as they listened to the end of Hester's conversation. Beulah kept trying to stretch her hand out to grab the phone, but Hester kept skipping to one side, shaking her head warningly at Beulah. 'Of course . . . she's here . . . so tall and the head off Beulah when she was her age . . . I know she has the height as well . . . yes . . . no trouble only a great support . . . she is a great nurse to poor old Beulah. Do you know, what would really suit her now would be to be a farmer's wife . . . what? . . . What's that? . . . no, I wouldn't say that at all.'

Beccy was angry, she wanted to grab the phone off Hester. Beulah gave Hester a furious look, but furious looks didn't work as well these days when she wasn't able to tower over Hester. Beulah would have got out of the wheelchair only she didn't want to appear too sprightly. Beccy wheeling her around was a great comfort. She didn't want them to think that she was capable of walking.

Hester's face dropped, she wandered over to the small hall window, winding the telephone cord around her fingers, her voice low and hesitant, 'Why? . . . are you that busy? . . . over

162

Christmas . . . shouldn't you be taking it easy? . . . What about Beccy? . . . do you want a word? . . .'

Beccy moved eagerly towards the phone, but Hester's voice dropped even further, her body was hooped over, almost cradling the phone. 'Right I'll tell her . . . bye for now . . . would you be able to ring back . . . at all . . . Leah . . . she's gone,' Hester finished, looking at Beulah and Beccy with bewilderment.

'You big stupid fool!' Beulah cried. 'Why didn't you put her on to me?

'I couldn't, she kept saying "hang on a minute, don't go!" What could I say to that? I couldn't go against her wishes.'

'You could, of course, tell her that you were handing her over to her direct relations.'

'It's not Hester's fault,' Beccy's black eyes were wet. 'I know what Mummy is like.'

'And do you think I don't?' Beulah pointed to the front door. 'Take me out now, before I go mad from thinking about the mess she's after making.' Beulah tried another withering look at Hester, but her position in the wheelchair put her at a disadvantage.

'Once Leah makes up her mind, that's it, there's nothing you can do or say,' Beccy shrugged as she wheeled the chair.

'I could have changed her mind for her. Does she not know that her mother is crippled. Did you not say one word about my arthritis?'

'I didn't get a chance, she didn't ask about you, anyway,' Hester flung back, before the hall door slammed.

Blaming Hester didn't help if Leah didn't care. Beulah was silent as the wheelchair rumbled up the garden path. They approached the still water-wheel. It was covered in moss.

'Isn't the mill lovely!' Beccy said, as she always said when they passed the silent water-mill.

163

'It is very run-down. It was lovely, once,' answered Beulah. The water-mill was an unfortunate structure, everybody in the whole world wanting to stop and admire it.

Could it really be true that Leah didn't care about her? Perhaps she had fussed over John too much, but that was because she was afraid that she would lose him. She did lose him. So she was right to have given him as much as she could when he was alive.

She had done lots of things for Leah too, but they were all forgotten about. All sorts of things were coming back to her now. She remembered teaching her *The Lord is my shepherd*, holding Leah for hours after a bee sting. Leah wouldn't let her out of her sight for the rest of the summer in case another bee got her. She had to be accompanied everywhere, even if it was to get a drink of water from the kitchen. It was very trying. Of course, Hester helped, too, but Beulah remembered that she hardly got a tap of work done with all the interruptions.

She taught Leah how to knit, guiding her chubby hands on the needles, when she must have been only four and a half. She knitted clothes for Leah's doll, Caroline. That red knitted coat with the pixie hat to match. The white lace baby dress with bootees. Of course John had liked to play with Caroline, too, so he got the use out of the clothes as well and of course Hester sewed even better dolls' clothes; that lime green gingham dress, so perfectly finished, you couldn't tell the inside from the outside. But still, Beulah had had her times with Leah. A lemon sleeveless dress, a bag made of knitted squares, fastened with a toggle from one of John's old duffle coats. Leah with an H-shaped frown stamped across her forehead, struggling to open the toggle, and close it and open it for hours in a circle of sun in the yard. Had Leah forgotten all that?

Beulah thought a lot about the Reverend Moylan and she thought about Louis. There was nothing else to do, she

164

couldn't wash now. She couldn't clean the place around her. She needed the comfort of order and activity, instead she saw piles of washing and Hester making wishy-washy efforts with half a basin of lukewarm water. Beccy made no effort to do any washing, she said that they had to get a washing machine.

Hester went off with Beccy one morning and bought a washing machine. *Zanussi*. Hester and Beccy said its name like an invocation. It rumbled and shook and trembled in the scullery. Hester was forever leaving things on top of it or against it. Saucepans or wire trays, they made the clatter ten times worse.

'Why do modern things have to be so noisy? I keep waking up and thinking it's the second coming!'

'Nan, it was Hester who insisted on getting a second-hand reconditioned one, trying to be thrifty. The real new ones are very quiet.'

'Don't think that I would have any more time for it if it was quiet, I wouldn't like it any better, work should make some noise so you know that you're doing it,' said Beulah.

She jumped again when the machine went into spin, 'Listen to that, it is like the opening-up of graves.'

The real truth was that Beulah didn't mind that much about the washing machine, after all. It was magical the way it washed the clothes, squeezing them far drier than Beulah could ever have managed. Beccy and Hester were like excited children, running in and out with soft fragrant sheets, drying them in front of the parlour fire during January. They washed blankets as well as sheets and the clothes were so well spun out by the rumbling machine, they dried quickly. Beulah thought about all those years she'd spent wringing until her wrists ached. It was a relief now not to have to worry about washing, and it was becoming a relief to think about the past she had tried to forget for so many years.

'Doesn't the whole place smell like a garden?' sighed Beccy,

165

one dark wintry afternoon when she and Beulah were sitting with two large cups of tea and a plate of pink tea-time wafers.

'I've no time for those fabric conditioners,' lied Beulah. 'Those unnatural smells.'

Beccy suddenly held her wrist under Beulah's nose. 'Do you like this perfume? I got it from a friend at Christmas.'

'It is nice,' Beulah thought it was breathtaking, the flowery perfume mixed with the cinnamon and salt and pears that was Beccy's own smell. They said that youth was wasted on the young; well, their smells definitely were wasted on them. Beulah never knew what she smelt like but she remembered young Joe Costello's grassy clean-bandages smell.

'Diorissimo,' said Beccy proudly. 'I thought you'd like it, because it is very old-fashioned.'

'It's not like anything I remember,' said Beulah. 'Of course we weren't allowed it, but Hester and I, we had a weakness for it. Margaret Costello, if she was down in Sheehan's, she would leave such a scent. I think it was Chanel. And Old Costello, bay rum. I would have given anything for Bertie to wear bay rum. It was the bee's knees.'

Beulah stopped for a moment as Beccy's face brightened up. Beccy wanted to know everything about what she called long ago and Beulah was always afraid that she might say too much. She blamed it on not being able to wash and scrub or belt sheets against the wall. The only way she could get things out her system now was to talk.

Beulah looked down at her hands. How could they have got knotted so quickly? Beccy was such a good listener, she couldn't help continuing, 'Joe Costello, now. When he was young he wore bay rum for a while, too.'

'Was he very handsome?'

'How would I have known a thing like that? All I knew was that he gave it up when he started going out with a girl he met in Kerry. Joe went off learning Irish on his holidays. His father

166

didn't like it, he looked down on all that stuff, *gaelgeoirs* and the GAA.'

'How do you know?'

'He told me.'

'Old Dr Costello?'

'Of course not. Joe. He began to grow a beard then, wore a greeny tweed jacket with a tin whistle in the inside pocket. I didn't like the beard on him,' Beulah stifled a sharp intake of breath. 'Old Nellie Sheehan said the learning Irish was a cod, that all the young doctors were doing it to try and get the best jobs. There was a job called the Junior Ad and you had to be really good at Irish to get it. But what did Joe need to get the Junior Ad for? Wasn't he going to take over his father's practice?'

'Can you remember other things about him?'

'I can remember lots of things about him, he had to get a special letter of permission from his bishop to allow him to study medicine at Trinity College.'

'Why?'

'Because Trinity was for the Protestants and Archbishop McQuaid didn't like Catholics going there. And I can remember him wearing green plus fours and driving a scooter when petrol was scarce.'

'But didn't he need to put petrol in the scooter.'

'How do I know?' Beulah burst out angrily. 'I was a Poleite. Maybe it was fashion, like the tin whistle and the girl in Kerry.'

'You don't seem to like the girl in Kerry.'

'Of course I liked her, isn't she Mrs Costello now?'

This was another lie. Beulah had spent the last forty years pretending that Mrs Costello didn't exist. It was easy most of the time. The Costellos didn't have any children and Mrs Costello kept away from the village. She was a thin stylish woman and she spent a lot of time in Dublin, doing stylish things, no doubt. She had a lot of family there and they said that she hated the country. Beulah thought that she was very plain but she never heard anyone else saying so. Alone with Joe Costello up at the surgery, it was easy to pretend he didn't have a wife.

'Mrs Costello,' said Hester, entering the room. 'I never heard her coming out with any Irish talk, or Joe either for that matter.'

'It was only a fad, Old Nellie Sheehan was sure of it even then. They were all congregating down in Kruger Kavanagh's outside Dingle. An excuse for a good time. The people with money pretending that they were only there to be talking Irish and growing beards.'

'I can't remember the beard at all,' Hester said.

'Well, I do,' insisted Beulah, she tried to straighten out her gnarled fingers. 'This talk is giving me more pain, give me a couple of tablets, the big white ones.'

Beccy went out to get water while Hester sat by Beulah, musing. 'I don't remember any rich people apart from the Costellos. Do you remember during the war years when there was no petrol and Dr Costello had a gas bag on top of his Morris 12? Do you remember the big balloon thing that burnt coke?'

'I do,' said Beulah, absent-mindedly. She was thinking about the first time she heard that Joe Costello had a girlfriend.

Chapter Sixteen

Red-hot needles tingled at the bottom of Beulah's fingers, her left knee was on fire, she might as well be in Hell with the pain that she was in.

Walking down the main street in town, past the shop girls with their perms stuck to the side of their heads like galvanised iron roofs, she had not wanted to see Joe in any shape or form, especially not with a wiry beard.

'Oh, where are you going?' he said. She could never have asked him where *he* was going, but that was because it meant far too much to her.

'I'm going to Mrs Tobin's about her book.'

'What happened to it?'

'I burnt it,' Beulah remembered how good she had felt, how Louis laid his hand proudly on her shoulder. The thin fan of ash that was all that was left of *The Walk of a Queen* when the fire burned out. She had been forgiven. Louis could have been hard on her, but he was a good Christian, *surely goodness and kindness shall follow me all the days of my life*. Nearly midnight, Beulah fired with good resolve, had wanted to blacklead the range on the spot only Louis stopped her. 'At least let me oil the wringer,' Beulah had begged before Louis firmly led her back to her room.

'It is against Poleite law to punish yourself,' Louis said. 'We are not Catholics.'

Louis had to move out because Shep took up too much room in their bed. Each night at eight o'clock, Louis filled two hot-water bottles, one for Shep and one for Beulah, and slipped them between their sheets. Shep the convalescent became Shep the gooseberry. Louis let Shep take his place every night, he indulged Beulah in every way, went down to Sheehan's for bags of sugar and gold-wrapped Crunchies. Loaves of white bread. Red lemonade heated in a saucepan over the range at bedtime. Goody for breakfast. Looking back, it seemed like heaven; no one telling her what to eat and when to eat it. No one telling her what to do. The crimson coals through the black bars of the range, the tick of the clock, the smell of hot lemonade. But it was an overheated room; Joe Costello haunting every dark corner. His double-breasted brown-striped suit, his polished brown shoes that shone with golden lights. His eyes, his face, the way he spoke about medicine. She was constantly seeing the room through his eyes, hearing Louis with his ears. She became more irritated with the way Louis picked up words and phrases from Danny Fox, 'As sure as God made gooseberries!'

That cold morning, the morning she met Joe Costello wearing his plus fours and his beard, the street was thronged with men driving their cattle to the mart; everything smelt of cows and cow dung. The cows groaned tragically. As Beulah looked at Joe, his figure seemed to shrink as if he was moving into the distance. Joe rattled change in his pocket, heartily, 'Did you burn it because it was about a convert?'

'No,' lied Beulah, looking at the width of his calves, not knowing whether she liked them or not. Seeing a man in plus fours was worse than seeing a man in a bathing suit. Not that Beulah had ever seen a man in a bathing suit, only Hester had described a picture that she had come across once, in a pattern book in the draper's.

'I didn't think it was a very good book.'

'Well,' said Joe, admiringly. 'You are someone with a bit of taste. I didn't like to say it to Mrs Tobin because she is the salt of the earth, you know, but that Annie Smithson is not a very good writer.'

'Have you read much of her?' Beulah asked, with her hand on the door of the chemist's shop.

'Are you trying to insult me?' Joe asked, evasively.

Beulah was unsure of herself, and she couldn't think of what to say about *The Walk of a Queen*, the book that she hadn't read. At the back of her mind, the memory of her black hair flowing over her shoulders while she sat on the black leatherette sofa was threatening to break in. She kept it back.

Joe gallantly held the door open for her and Mrs Tobin, looking thrilled, came out from behind her mahogany counter with her soft white hands outstretched, 'Well, if it isn't Beulah, what did himself think of our hairstyle?'

Beulah stared at Mrs Tobin's head with its silver hair gleaming like a crown. She took an unsteady foot forwards and wavered.

'Look at her bad colour! She's going to faint!'

Joe caught hold of a slim wooden chair with a round back and guided Beulah into it. She could feel his hands warm next to her cold ones.

'Have you got news for us?' Mrs Tobin asked while Beulah watched Mrs Tobin's silver crown waving in the air.

'News, what kind of news?' Beulah asked, wonderingly.

'Oh, you know, when you are just married,' whispered Mrs Tobin. '*That* kind of news.'

'I don't know what you are talking about,' Beulah said, crossly, wondering if Mrs Tobin was hinting something about her relationship with Joe.

171

'Oh, love, I would not upset you for the world,' Mrs Tobin began to chafe Beulah's hands. 'What did I go saying that for? What news is right! I must be off my head, what kind of an *oinseach* am I?'

'I don't know, I don't understand Irish,' Beulah gasped for breath and Mrs Tobin's silky fingers began to unbutton the pearly buttons at the neck of her wedding dress.

'And you are right too, all that Irish business is only a fad, look at the state of that fellow with his beard, he's like Jeremiah O'Donovan Rossa gone mad.'

Joe started when Mrs Tobin pointed at him. Beulah could see his confidence draining out of him. 'Go and get a glass of water and make yourself useful!'

Joe dragged his feet, he didn't take his eyes off the small v of skin at the neck of Beulah's dress. Beulah remembered another drawing room where Joe had opened the neck of her dress to put the stethoscope against her skin. She wondered if he remembered it. She felt herself blush.

'It is all right, Joe, she's going to be okay,' Mrs Tobin called out. 'The roses are coming back into her cheeks. What a lovely complexion! She's like a nun with the lovely skin. Hasn't paint and powder the rest of us ruined!'

'I haven't got your book for you,' said Beulah, her eyes fixed on Joe's eyes fixed on her open collar. She hoped Louis was still at the cattle mart. That he wouldn't see Joe leaving the shop.

'I knew you would want to keep it! And there's no problem there as long as I'm keeping the librarian supplied with bromides.'

'Mrs Tobin!' said Joe, drawing his eyes away from from the inch of skin at Beulah's throat.

'Have you heard about himself down in Kerry?' Mrs Tobin tossed her silver crown at Joe. 'A right *gaelgeoir* we have here with his *ceart go leor* and his Irish dancing. Scaling Mount Brandon he was, last weekend. And who was he trying to impress?' Mrs Tobin paused dramatically, as Beulah stared at her bloodshot eyes. 'Would it have been someone called Mary, by any chance? Someone called Mary from Kerry?'

Mrs Tobin looked at Beulah's stricken face. 'I was disappointed myself, in fact I didn't believe the rumours until I saw their photograph in the paper. Listowel Races, if you don't mind, and she is a right "Rose of Tralee". Isn't she, Joe?'

'I think I am going to get sick,' said Beulah.

But Mrs Tobin had enough of acting nurse to Beulah. 'We'll be having wedding bells, any day now, isn't that right, Joe?'

There were roses everywhere. They were back in Joe's cheeks now too. Mrs Tobin went on, 'I want to give Beulah a nice little book for her bedside locker! Have you ever heard of *Knocknagow* otherwise known as *The Homes of Tipperary*? Of course you mightn't want to read all that stuff about the famine and workhouses, it's very depressing. Now what *you* would really like is the Baroness Orczy.'

'I must go now,' said Beulah but she didn't want to leave Joe in spite of the plus fours and the wild beard and the Rose of Tralee. She was sick with jealousy and longing. She wanted Joe to say it wasn't true even though he had every right to be courting *gaelgeoirs* when he was an eligible batchelor and she was married. Joe leant forward and fastened the three pearly buttons on the neck of her dress.

'Now, I want to know, I'll be very interested to see what you think of the Baroness Orczy. You will just love the Scarlet Pimpernel!' A bad sweet smell was coming from Mrs Tobin. Joe's nimble hands burned against her neck, he had said that he really wanted to be a surgeon but his father wouldn't allow him.

'Oh those nimble-fingered butchers!' The Reverend Moylan swayed in his glittery sugar-coated suit among the sunbeams in Kingston's parlour. Ranting against doctors.

'There's a verse, have you ever heard it? "We seek him here,

173

we seek him there . . ." said Mrs Tobin as she went into the back to look for the books.

Mrs Tobin returned, looking puzzled, her hair was untidy. 'Isn't it strange? I can't lay my hands on them now. Do you know that verse at all, Joe? "Is he in heaven – Is he in hell? That demmed, elusive pimpernel!" '

Joe looked embarrassed, he didn't answer Mrs Tobin. He followed Beulah who was moving to the door with her head down. Beulah was afraid that she was going to cry.

Outside on the street, Beulah ran towards the trap in relief. Louis still hadn't returned from the mart. How she didn't slip on the street or collide with anyone was a miracle. Her heart thudded as she sat on top of the trap. If Louis or, even worse, the Reverend Moylan, had seen her consorting with that awful woman!

Across the street, she saw Joe pause for a moment. He picked up one of his pigskin gloves which had fallen on the ground. She thought that he was going to ignore her and walk on. Joe dusted his glove and crossed over the street. He looked up as he passed her sitting high above him on the trap. 'Are you all right, now?'

'I am not all right!'

'Are you sleeping at night?' Joe asked.

'Of course I am not!' Beulah burst out angrily. At the end of the street she could see the brim of Louis's hat.

'Do you still go down to the water-wheel?' Joe asked, fingering his glove.

Beulah wondered if Joe could see Louis, who was still at least a hundred and fifty yards away. She took a deep breath, 'If you want to see the wheel working, you could come down in the evening. That is when I go down there. Watching the mill, watching the wheel go round, it is better than any sleeping medicine.'

'Well, you haven't tried any medicine yet,' Joe smiled and

went on, 'But I must get up to see that water-wheel some time, I would really like to see it working.'

'It will be working tonight,' Beulah said. Joe looked embarrassed. She didn't want to hear his refusal, so she cracked the whip, trotting Sally up towards Louis who broke into a smile under his hat. He did not see Joe Costello.

Chapter Seventeen

Hester was talking to Beccy in the kitchen. Beccy didn't understand why Beulah continued to see Joe Costello, if it was against her religion.

'Isn't it true that they just keep giving out drugs anyway, she's not getting any better, why doesn't she go back to being a proper Poleite?

Hester's lower lip began to shake. 'The things we saw when we were growing up. I remember an old tramp that used to come, with things like cauliflowers growing out of the side of his nose. He used to creep around the side of the school and frighten the children, standing there, with his tumours swaying in the breeze. We used to call him the man with all the noses.'

Hester was quiet for a few minutes, as she remembered the man with all the noses. 'Poor old man and we all ran away from him! It is a very hard thing to do without a doctor. I can't expect it from Beulah.'

'But you don't go yourself.'

'But I'm fine,' said Hester.

Beulah woke up then and they heard Beulah shouting from the parlour. Hester had moved the wheelchair to the window. Beulah slept a lot of the time now, Joe Costello had her on a variety of painkillers and sleeping tablets. Somehow, they got through the long winter, the garden was dancing with pinks and yellows and sap green. The washing line hung with a row of purplish-grey garments. Beulah rapped the floor with her stick and Beccy came running in breathless, her hands covered in earth.

'I don't want to see your handiwork. I'm telling you now.'

'Nan, is it the washing line you are talking about? That's the old stuff that was turned into dusters. Hester thought they needed to be boiled first. She said that was what you would do.'

'Isn't it great now to have Hester deciding what I would do! Isn't it, just!'

But really, Beulah was touched that anyone would want to do what she did. Even though she was sure that her laws of washing and housekeeping were absolute and gospel, there was not one other thing she had done that was right. She would have liked to have done right but it seemed impossible. God played with her like he'd played with Job. *My bones are pierced in me in the night season: and my sinews take no rest. By the great force of my disease is my garment changed: it bindeth me about as the collar of my coat . . . I cry unto thee and thou dost not hear me: I stand up and thou regardest me not.*

A week, that was all that John had lasted. Antibiotics or brandy, what did it matter now? He was fated to die. John couldn't even remember how he got the cut on his ankle. It festered for two days before he even noticed. He was blown away that easy, like a ball of fluff from a dandelion.

Beulah always thought it was the rat poison. If she had allowed him to have a dog, John mightn't have been laying out the poison. It came in a yellow box, there was a picture of a rat with very long teeth on the front of the box. She burnt what was left over in a fit of rage after John died. She would have welcomed a whole tribe of plague-carrying rats, but the rats disappeared with John. He had said that it was the strongest poison you could get.

John had been laying out the rat poison in the barn, Beulah

called him for his tea but he said that he wanted to get finished with it in one go. He was twenty-six but he seemed as young as Louis. White skin and pink cheeks, his broad-brimmed black hat shoved to the back of his pole. His forehead shone with sweat. It was hot, but he never took off his heavy Poleite clothes. He was never interested in getting married, Beulah had always been pleased about that. She never asked herself why.

The Reverend Moylan tried as best he could, but the Reverend's vigour was draining away with age. He was losing his mesmerising power and he had no successor. John visited him most evenings, he was keen to be a proper Poleite. 'Mama, when he's gone there will be no one to tell us what to do.'

The Reverend spoke at length to Beulah in private about the mistakes that he had made, 'I can tell you, Beulah, because I know you're not perfect. I would never say a word to your mother, it would upset her too much.'

'You see, the thing is, I should have got married. I thought at the time I was keeping my strength for the flock. And now my flock are leaving me, two by two. An aspirin here, a disprin there and the next thing it's chest X-rays and antibiotics. There's no stopping them. If I had a son, he would have continued the ministry. He would have had to do his duty. Or maybe he wouldn't,' the Reverend Moylan's voice trailed away, uncertainly.

'But still, it's great to be able to talk to someone, I could talk to your poor mother. She was a saint. Of course, I'd never upset her with this kind of talk.' The Reverend dropped his eyes on to his hands and then raised them again to Beulah, looking ashamed. 'But I wasn't honest with you the first time. The real reason I didn't want to marry was I wanted a young girl and I only got the chance with widows. Twice I was offered widows, but I refused. I had the Bible to back me up and I quoted from the laws and ordinances concerning the priests. The Book of Leviticus.' The Reverend Moylan cleared his throat sternly,

'*A widow or a divorced woman, or profane, or an harlot, these shall he not take: but he shall take a virgin of his own people to wife.*' The Reverend looked even more ashamed. His voice grew small and pleading, 'But was it so very bad anyway to want a young woman?'

The morning that Beulah and John had gone to town to get the poison, they were still using the trap and the people seemed to stare more than usual. It was sunny and the town was bursting with long-haired young men and women. Beulah and John trotted through the main street, conspicuous and black among all the different-coloured flared jeans, the paisleys and the flowers. As they stopped outside the hardware shop, a girl walked past them. She looked up into John's face and smiled at him. Every tooth in the girl's head was perfect and white. Beulah had never seen anything like her, she was so beautiful and different with her flawless olive skin, the way her short dark curls clung to her perfect head. She was familiar as well, some child from the town that had suddenly grown up. John's face was scarlet under his black hat and when Beulah looked into his eyes they were full of misery. He watched the girl walk away. She wore a tight-fitting white T-shirt and jeans. The word *Peace* was embroidered on one of her back pockets, the word *Love* on the other. Beulah was astounded that such a modest face would have those words written on her pockets.

'That must be the eldest one of the Hanlons, I'd hardly recognise her,' Beulah said to John as he jumped off the trap to get the poison. He didn't answer and his face was as red as an apple. Beulah wondered if he knew the girl but she didn't see how John and Teresa Hanlon could have known each other, when she was always watching over John.

A few years later she heard Nellie Sheehan talking about Teresa Hanlon and how she had gone off the rails in London.

179

'Drugs and every bad thing you could think of! Of course, she was too beautiful, that was her problem,' Nellie said.

It mightn't have been the rat poison, it could have been anything. He had no resistance, by the time Beulah was bathing the festering cut with salt and water, he was feverish and sick. He was in bed for five days, going down rapidly. Hester and Beulah took turns by the bed, cold flannels on his forehead, hot drinks. Everything happened so fast, his ankle was a ball of pus. They had to force the water in a trickle down his throat. Beulah wondered if he would mention Teresa Hanlon, but he did not. He raved and called to some imaginary dog. It made Beulah's hair stand on end to hear him clicking his tongue and patting the air.

Hester asked Beulah to open the Bible at random, maybe it would give them advice, guide them in some way. The pages fell open on the Book of Samuel and then Hester was very sorry that she'd asked Beulah to open the Bible.

And Absalom met the servants of David. And Absalom rode upon a mule and the mule went under the thick boughs of a great oak and his head caught hold of the great oak and he was taken up between the heaven and the earth and the mule that was under him was taken away.

For five days in bed, John hung by the string of his life like Absalom hanging by his hair from the oak.

Then said Joab, I may not tarry thus with thee. And he took three darts in his hand, and thrust them through the heart of Absalom while he was yet alive in the midst of the oak . . . the king was much moved and went up to the chamber over the gate, and wept: and as he went, thus he said, Oh my son Absalom, my son, my son Absalom! Would God I had died for thee, O Absalom, my son, my son!

Beulah felt that she couldn't call the doctor. John himself was a devout Poleite, it was one thing to transgress laws herself but another thing entirely to corrupt her son. In the end it was

Hester who suggested it, and by then it was far too late. It was like it had happened yesterday, taking the sheet and wrapping it around him, he seemed so small in death. As she kissed his hands goodbye, for a moment, she thought she could hear Shep barking in the distance.

Shep jumped up from the bed, immediately sniffing and huffing. Looking for a walk. 'Get down! Get back! Shhhhhh!' Beulah said. Louis had driven them home from town in silence, she could hardly bear to speak. She was wishing that Joe hadn't grown that beard. She was sick from beards, looking at them all her life, on every man's face that was close to her. Bertie, Reverend Moylan, Louis. She had loved Joe's smooth face. She did not want to believe in Mrs Tobin. She did not want to believe in this Mary person. Mrs Tobin had sounded hysterical: Mary from Kerry, the Rose of Tralee.

But Joe might come to see the mill. She had asked him and he said he was interested in the water-wheel. Outside in the darkness, the air smelt free, the water-wheel made the best music and there was no Mary out there.

Beulah wrapped a thick linen sheet around her long white nightdress. Everything about her was white apart from her black eyes and her black hair. She could feel every ounce of colour gone from her cheeks.

Shep gambolled under Beulah's feet but Beulah climbed over her to get through the door, trying to push Shep back as she did so. The dog whined and whimpered. Beulah pushed her back and slammed the door. Shep yelped.

'Blast you too,' said Beulah. It was the only curse she knew. What Bertie said, to the hammer, once, when it had hit his thumb.

Shep continued to whimper as Beulah made her way along the corridor. 'Blast you, blast you!' What a selfish dog Shep was, trying to ruin her one chance of happiness.

181

Beulah stopped along the corridor outside Louis's door. There was no sound. Boldly, for she had to be sure, she pushed open the door and crept over to the side of the bed, jumping nervously at each whine that came down the corridor from her bedroom. Louis lay sleeping on his back like a king. His eyes were shut and his breathing shallow. He smelt fresh and clean. When she was sure that he was sleeping, Beulah hurried out of the room.

The smell of lilac was heavy as she walked through the garden. There might have been a bit of a chill in the air, especially at Hollywood farm where the house lay so low. *Down in a holla*, Danny Fox always said. Beulah remembered feeling hot. Nearly feverish. She was always hot when she was angry. And she was very angry with Shep.

Chapter Eighteen

How could hands curl up, get gnarled so quickly? Beulah thought that she had lost everything and then she lost a whole lot more. 'Once you have your health . . .' Old Mrs Sheehan's voice would trail off significantly. Old Mrs Sheehan was obsessed with health. The Reverend Moylan said she was obsessed even before she ever got the arthritis.

Mrs Sheehan got gold injections for her arthritis, they were all the go then. Beulah used to imagine the gold pouring in a thin liquid filament through Old Mrs Sheehan's bloodstream. Old Mrs Sheehan maintained that John was sickly, he needed a tonic; Beulah said that it wasn't allowed.

'You don't have to let on to anyone, do you?' said Old Mrs Sheehan, putting a twiggy arthritic forefinger to the side of her nose. 'I'll write the name down for you, Dr Collis Brown's Chlorodyne. That's the stuff! A couple of swigs of that a day and he'll be a topper.'

Six-year-old John was peaky, his parchment-coloured forehead barely reached the top of the counter and he strained to look over at Old Mrs Sheehan who sat inside the counter on her special high-backed stool. Old Mrs Sheehan unscrewed the jar of barley sugar twists and gave one to John. John nearly dropped the barley sugar, afraid of Old Mrs Sheehan's deformed fingers.

*   *   *

Nellie Sheehan liked to hold forth on health matters too, but she couldn't do it while Sheila was around because she might be contradicted. Even though she was highly cynical about surgeons. 'They're like tradesmen, the first thing they'll do when they look in is to make little of the last man's work.' She had had many unsuccessful operations on her knee

'How do they look into the knee?' asked Beulah. 'Is it an X-ray or what?'

'Oh, I've had *them* too. Don't talk to me about the arthrogram and the squelchy noise after they inject the dye. They make you bend your knee back and forth and it sounds like a leaky wellington.'

Those were the days when Beulah was on her feet, but she didn't want to talk about such things anymore. Now, she sat in her wheelchair while Beccy roamed around the shop ticking off items from a list. In the old days you didn't get to pick out anything yourself, Old Mrs Sheehan and Nellie handed everything out over the counter. They wrapped everything up themselves too. In 1976 the big counter was moved back and the customers picked out their own goods. As a child, Beulah had longed to be weighing and wrapping in Sheehan's shop as much as she had longed to be behind the counter of the post office, carefully tearing out rows of stamps along the perforated margin, licking labels. Melting sealing wax and pressing the seal firmly into the warm soft mass. Or wearing a nurse's uniform with an upside-down watch and a stethoscope.

But once the customers were let in, it wasn't as nice at all. The brown paper bags, the sugar and the scoop were all gone. Along with the sweet jars and the rows and rows of plug tobacco, Garryowen and Clarke's nugget, the little boxes of Robin starch. The boxes of smudgy 'blue' for washing clothes. The golden-wood till disappeared with the old wide counter and Nellie Sheehan sat behind an electric cash register. Now it was packets and boxes and tins. See-through flimsy plastic bags.

Beulah let on that she couldn't find things so that Nellie or Sheila would have to come outside and find them for her. Sheila didn't like that, she wanted to stay sitting behind the new cash register, ringing on it.

'There's too much choice nowadays,' said Nellie Sheehan. 'I met Sean Power from Churchtown the other day, do you remember him, Beulah? With the turned-in toes? He told me he had landed out ninety pounds, imagine, to a herbalist up in Cork. He can't have beef or dairy products or cigarettes.'

'That's not much of a choice,' said Beulah.

'Was it Chinese herbs?' asked Beccy.

'I couldn't tell you, between reflexology and psychotherapy and the whole lot I get very mixed up. Sheila could tell you now, if you had a day or two to be sitting down with her.'

'The Chinese are supposed to be very good, though,' Beccy said.

'Well, they've been at it a while, I've heard. Their medicine is two and a half times as old as the Bible. Whether that is a good thing or not I don't know. All I know is that I couldn't be landing out ninety pounds a go on top of the paying out to the Voluntary Health Insurance. Are you in the Voluntary Health, Beulah?'

'No,' said Beulah, shortly, glad that Hester wasn't around to be keeling over at the sums of money that were being talked about. Even Beulah felt it was shameful.

After a few weeks Beulah developed a rash, she didn't mention the Book of Job to the others but it was never far from her mind. *Skin for skin, yea, all that a man hath he will give for his life . . . So went Satan forth from the presence of the Lord, and smote Job with sore boils from the sole of his foot to the crown of his head.*

It started as a rash under her ring and then it spread. 'I wouldn't mind but you haven't had your hands in washing powder for about two months,' said Hester. Beulah was in an agony of painful itch but it was Hester that got most bothered. Hester was sure that it was contagious and rushed around disinfecting cups and towels. In fear for herself, she lost all sympathy for Beulah. And Beulah was powerless in the wheelchair. The whole house stank of calamine lotion, TCP and Dettol.

Hester called in Danny Fox to ask for his opinion. 'He knows a lot about the old cures and that's what you should have stuck to instead of going up to Dr Costello's surgery. God knows what you've picked up there, not to mind the county hospital,' Hester shuddered.

'This way, Danny,' Hester called out callously when Danny Fox came knocking at the door.

'Don't let him see my knees!'

Danny was not allowed into the parlour but there was a lot of muttering out in the corridor. She could hear him mentioning his mother, saying that Maggie Fox had had something similar.

'Goat's milk, now,' said Danny and Beulah winced at his high nasal voice.

Beccy and Hester seemed to agree about goat's milk.

'It can't do any harm,' said Beccy.

'Anything natural,' said Hester.

Beulah listened to Danny's footsteps going off to get the goat's milk and she took in a deep breath as Beccy turned the handle of the parlour door, 'That man comparing me with his mother who was taken off to hospital, crawling with lice.'

'Beulah, we never knew for sure if she had lice or not,' said Hester.

'I knew that she had lice, I had reason to,' muttered Beulah. 'But I am not going to start drinking goat's milk at this hour of my age. I never touched it all my life and I am not about to start now. Could you imagine the filthy containers Danny Fox is handling!'

'He is getting it from some woman out beyond Farren,'

186

Hester said. 'Don't you know I was sure to check that she bottles it herself.'

'How do we know that he won't start tasting it himself?' said Beulah. 'Anyway, it is time for my appointment with Joe Costello.'

Beulah's mood continued to worsen, what she hated most of all was not being able to go to see Joe Costello on her own. Beccy was driving and then Hester got into the car as well, 'I feel like the spin,' she said, avoiding Beulah's angry glare.

When they got outside the house, Danny Fox was still there, his skinny leg up on a tree stump, surveying the orchard. He wore a huge grey overcoat fastened with one button over his chest, it flapped open to show a dark greasy grey suit underneath.

'I think he got dressed up to see you, Beulah,' Beccy said.

'He's like Johnny Forty Coats,' said Hester, adding, 'Wouldn't you nearly think he has the coat open on purpose to show the suit?'

Danny looked at them and gave a salute, giving the coat a tweak to make it fall open. When he was sure they were all looking at him, he looked away with a careless air.

'Keep smiling at him,' said Hester, giving Danny a wave. 'We want him to get that goat's milk.'

'Oh yes,' said Beulah. 'The goat's milk that I am not going to drink!'

Two days later, Beccy went to collect the goat's milk.

'I know she won't touch it, you know,' said Danny as he opened the door. 'She won't have anything to do with me.'

'Why not?' asked Beccy, peering around the dark kitchen.

'Oh sure, now,' said Danny. 'You know yourself.' He started humming. The walls were bare except for a calendar with a picture of a horse. A bundle of old lottery tickets was wedged behind the clock on the mantelpiece. The room smelt of

187

woodsmoke, rashers and cat. A moulting cat sat on an old car seat by the fire. Beccy went to rub its back and then gasped at the open wound on its leg.

'That's Queenie,' said Danny, smiling.

'But her leg!'

'Oh she had the bad leg all right, but she's flying now.'

'Has she been to the vet?' asked Beccy, as the cat groaned in a low voice.

'Imagine, she is nearly sixteen years of age,' Danny went on, ignoring Beccy's question. 'Would you have a cup of tea, would you?'

'Okay,' said Beccy, uncertainly looking for somewhere to sit down as Danny began to throw a pile of *Irish Independents* and *Old Moore's Almanacs* off a rickety armchair. He patted an old flat cushion, 'Would you like a Wagon Wheel with it? Do you like Wagon Wheels?'

The end of the kitchen table was beside the armchair, Beccy sat with her back to the cat as Danny opened a cupboard beside the fire. He took out three Wagon Wheels and rolled them across the oilcloth. There was another growl from the cat.

'Oh, listen to herself,' said Danny. 'She's looking for her Wagon Wheel. She is pure mad about them.'

Danny's tea was scalding hot, golden and perfect. Beccy unwrapped her Wagon Wheel and, keeping her back to Queenie, who could be heard loudly guzzling her own Wagon Wheel, asked again, 'But why does Beulah not talk to you?'

'Well, Leah was a great friend of mine always, she used to come down here playing Forty-Five and did she ever tell you about the donkey?'

'I remember the donkey,' Beccy said, her face lighting up.

'I forgot about that, weren't you down here yourself you must have been about two. Of course, Leah never forgot me and she was as bad as yourself with the questions. She didn't get

188

on with Beulah and it was all John with Beulah, which was wrong. It was very wrong. Leah felt neglected.'

'Oh, she never stops talking about that, I know all about *that*,' said Beccy, in a bored voice. 'I want to know about Beulah and what is the big mystery about grandfather.'

'And how would I know in the name of God? Sure, Beulah would hardly tell me. And anyway what mystery? Isn't every death a mystery? Louis was a very good man, God rest his soul. And didn't God send two children in the one act to replace him. Do you know they were the first set of identical twins in the parish for seven years. The excitement was mighty. And that old minister, Reverend Moylan, he was as happy as a lamb with two mothers.'

Danny's eyes kept sliding nervously towards the cat. Beccy was sorry that she had mentioned the vet. It was clear that any vet would have Queenie put down on the spot and that was exactly what Danny could not face.

'You are the spit of Beulah at your age, do you know that?'

'Hester says so all right, but there's no photographs.'

'She could be very kind too, you know, Beulah.' Danny seemed to like saying the name and he pursed up his lips every time he said it. 'Beulah helped me with my mother. You see, my mother suffered desperate from ulcers, and doctors were expensive then. You'd have to pay them to come out and they wouldn't come out cheap, I can tell you. We didn't have the money.'

'Beulah used to dress my mother's leg every evening. Your great-grandmother now, Han Kingston, gave her homemade ointment to rub in and Beulah used to tear up old sheets after boiling them and it was not an easy job.'

'No,' agreed Beccy, looking at Queenie's leg.

'Ah, Beulah was a Trojan now, she did a lot for my mother. She often stayed here to mind her, before she went to hospital for the last time, God rest her soul. Did you ever know that

189

now? I'm telling you, if I hadn't Beulah here to keep an eye on her when I went to the mart and the creamery, and once I went off to Listowel races, the mother would have gone a whole pile earlier. And there's not many people knows about it, because Beulah was far too modest to let it be known.'

'Gone where?' asked Beccy.

'Gone to heaven,' Danny said impatiently, and then added, 'I hope,' in a lower voice. He sat looking down at his gnarled hands folded in his lap. 'That was all a long time ago. God, Beulah was beautiful, then. Of course you're the image of her but, I hope you don't mind me saying so, you are not as good-looking. It could be the clothes, I suppose. She wore beautiful clothes,' Danny scratched the back of his filthy neck. 'There was a very nice grey frock if I remember rightly.'

When she got home, Beccy spoke to Hester about Danny's cat. 'It's absolute cruelty keeping the cat in such agony and it's going to die anyway, it's sixteen for God's sake!' Hester said it was a domestic affair, they couldn't possibly interfere. Beccy asked about the old Poleite clothes.

'I think I still have some of John's clothes above in the attic,' Hester's lower lip trembled and she seemed weak and breathless climbing the steep stairs to the attic. Beccy was dying to see the clothes but she felt obliged to ask Hester if she was able for the stairs. Hester said that she was dying to see the clothes herself. 'I've never really had reason to take them out before.'

Beccy held her breath as Hester pushed in the low creaky door, her eyes sparkled as she looked in, anticipating the room full of ancient treasures and mementos. To her surprise, she saw that it was empty except for a small grey trunk. The bare boards were swept clean, there wasn't as much as a cobweb.

'Sure, Beulah wouldn't allow any dust or clutter,' Hester said. 'She puts everything out for the rubbish man and that's the end of it, except once, didn't she catch Danny Fox going through the bin. There was a desperate fight between them. He always obeys Beulah unless he has drink taken. He gets very cheeky then and I don't like to listen to him. Twelve o'clock at night and I had my head under the bedclothes and my fingers in my ears.'

Hester's eyes were watery as she brought John's clothes out of the trunk. They'd been carefully wrapped with mothballs and lemon-coloured tissue twenty-five years before.

'Good material, you see,' said Hester, fingering the fine black cloth. 'It lasts forever. People do not realise that nowadays. You can't get stuff like this anymore.' Hester's eyes were still watery, but no tears fell, 'I am not saying this because I was his aunt, but he was a very special boy. Kind and gentle, you know. He had more sympathy in him than Leah. They were very different.'

'But weren't they identical? Danny Fox told me that they were,' asked Beccy. 'Or was it just their physical appearance?'

'Danny Fox!' said Hester. 'He doesn't know the meaning of the word identical. He is always using words and he doesn't know the meaning of them. Leah and John were like chalk and cheese. Leah was dark and he was fair, but they loved each other dearly.'

'Danny Fox said they were the first set of identical twins to be born in the parish for seven years.'

'Well, I don't know about the seven years and they certainly were not identical, but people were excited. It was a big thing. And even the infidels would come up to us and say "Isn't it great for Beulah, now." Everyone thought it was an awful tragedy, Louis's death!'

'Was Beulah pleased?'

'Of course she must have been,' said Hester as she put the pile of black clothes onto Beccy's lap. 'But she was tired for a long time and I suppose she was still in shock when the twins were born. The Reverend Moylan was delighted though.'

'Poor old man,' Hester sighed. 'The Reverend died five weeks after John. He was fading anyway, but after that he went out like a candle.'

'Poor man,' echoed Beccy as she shook out the old clothes. She tried them on in front of the mirror. Hester didn't seem to mind.

'The material is so soft and falls perfectly,' said Beccy.

'You see, I am telling you there is great quality in the old materials, that was Louis's old coat and I altered it.'

Beccy's long black plaits fell down from under the wide-brimmed hat, the black coat was loose and wide. She looked Jewish. She thought it was nice. *I am black but comely, O ye daughters of Jerusalem, as the tents of Kedar, as the curtains of Solomon.*

Hester told Beccy how the Reverend Moylan knew every psalm off by heart. Beccy began to memorise the Song of Solomon. *I sat down under his shadow with great delight and his fruit was sweet to my taste.* Beccy read the Bible, an old small black one that belonged to Louis. Beulah said she didn't know how Beccy didn't get put off by the smell of mildew and it got worse every time she turned a page. But Beccy said she liked that smell. She sniffed at the pages and then sniffed at the Diorissimo in the crevice of her elbow. She read on expectantly.

Chapter Nineteen

Neither the Reverend Moylan nor Bertie nor Han nor Hester ever knew how Louis had died. Joe Costello was the soul of discretion and Beulah depended on that.

Beulah sat down by the mill on that Friday night after the cattle fair. The sky was as black as the blacklead she used on the Stanley range. No stars, no moon, swathes of slate clouds drawn across.

Making her way down the garden path, past the stream (so noisy she was afraid that it would wake Louis), Beulah was half ashamed of what Joe Costello might think of her. On her right she could see the high stone wall that divided Kingston's land from Fox's. The noise of the wheel was deafening. She thought of Hell. The Reverend Moylan always said that Hell was a noisy place. 'They never stop clamouring down there!'

Beside the mill was a narrow bench, its wooden slats rotten with age. A splinter went under her fingernail and she plucked it out quickly. She had been nervous of splinters since she was a child. Bertie said if you didn't pull them out quick, you could get an infection and die. Han took splinters out with a huge darning needle. She ran the needle under boiling hot water, then plunged it into the affected finger. She did it for Beulah and Bertie and Hester. Han never seemed to get splinters herself. Hester and Beulah hated the sight of that needle but no one ever cried out. It would have been a sign of weakness. It would have been considered selfish.

Beulah crushed the half rotten splinter between her finger and thumb. She was caught in a mixture of fear and excitement. She hardly ever sat on this seat. She had lied to Joe Costello because she was desperate to meet him. The bench was near the wheel, sometimes it seemed as if the wheel would strike the bench and she almost ducked. The wheel kept turning its heavy relentless circle. Now and then, Beulah felt the spray cold on her face. Unable to go back, she closed her eyes very tight and pulled her knees up under her thick white gown. A late train rattled through the bottom of the next field. The noise was sharp in the air like a bird call or a signal.

She did not have to wait long but if he hadn't come, she would have stayed until morning. She was incapable of going back into the house. He approached from behind. She heard him stumble, but she kept her eyes shut. If she opened her eyes, he would disappear like a dream.

The first thing he touched was her hair, unravelling her plait, tingles ran everywhere like rivers on a map. As her hair fell to her knees, she thought that she heard him moan. She did not like the sound of it. She pretended that she hadn't heard. She held her breath.

The reek of lilacs was heavy like a drug. He smelt sweet too, his back as smooth as a baby's and narrower than she expected when she put her arms around him. Strange and familiar, like a dream. There were drums in her head and her body. She kept her eyes tightly shut.

As long as her eyes were shut, she felt graceful. He was gentle at the beginning. He smelt of apples and pears, of Swan soap. The very same Swan soap that sat in the brown and pink soap dish on the chest of drawers in her bedroom. Swan soap was floating soap. *The Soap that Floats* said the advertisement in Sheehan's shop.

194

Beulah had never had a bath, she had often wondered what it would be like to lie down, with a floating bar of soap riding the waves and the ripples. Poleites discouraged baths. 'A filthy habit!' Han said. 'Wallowing in mud!'

Beulah had been trained and had become addicted to early morning washes with icy water in front of an open window. So she was not afraid of the cold. She was able to stand with the folds of her nightdress around her waist and more folds thrown around her shoulders, her long legs bare and trembling. The familiar smell of Swan soap rising from his soft beard, her eyes sealed.

Bertie asked Beulah once if she was brave or if she was foolhardy. She never answered because she wasn't sure what foolhardy meant. If it meant a hard fool then she was sure she was foolhardy. Bertie had made them a swing when they were children. It hung from a branch that straddled a ditch and when Hester and Beulah sat on it they swung over and back between two fields. Hester was afraid when the rope creaked, she slowed down and peered up at it, anxiously. When Beulah was conscious of the rope creaking, she shut her eyes and swung harder.

As Beulah screwed her eyes shut, he put his hands over her eyes. His hands were small, slightly callused at the tips. Her heart gave a jolt. She had thought often enough about kissing his forehead, his temples and the side of his jaw, but she couldn't do it now, not after feeling those hands.

It was like icy morning washes but it was more painful. And unlike early morning washes, it was shameful. She had done wrong in the first place, coming out like this. What did she expect? How could she possibly object? She thought that she would break as he pushed into her, he made an awful sound. He kept his mouth over hers, it was very hard to breathe. There was a damp coldness between her legs and in the pit of her stomach as he pulled her nightdress down and kissed her closed eyelids. She didn't move, just kept her eyes screwed tight to keep back the tears. The footsteps went away, she heard that stumble again as she knelt on the damp ground searching blindly for her hairpins. She found three hairpins and managed to get her hair back into some kind of loop on the nape of her neck.

Beulah walked heavily back to the house, she saw the house and Louis's dark window. She didn't care about him now. Awake or asleep. A fierce stinging pain went through her body. She would not give in to tears. She knew what she needed. She needed water and soap. The latch was still up on the door. It moved noiselessly before her but she needed noise to relieve her of the pain so she banged it shut behind her. The pain was everywhere. The smell of lilac made her sick. Why hadn't she listened to Shep's warning? And now she hated Shep.

Pushing open the bedroom door she bumped into Shep's body, lying on the floor, tense and worried. Relieved, the dog threw herself against Beulah, barking. Beulah shushed and tried to put her hand over Shep's mouth to muzzle her, but Shep broke away yelping.

'And stay away, then' said Beulah, angrily, checking to see if there was water in the jug. She poured it in quickly, splashing herself and Shep, who crept back, trying to get close to her knee.

'Get away,' Beulah cuffed Shep across the head. Shep slithered on the floorboards trying to get away from Beulah's new sharp hand, new sharp voice.

When Beulah was scrubbed and smelling of soap once more, she ran her mind back over the things that had been done to her. She closed her eyes because she just couldn't bear Shep looking at her. Shep had grown up with her. It was worse than Han or Bertie finding out, having to look at those brown eyes of conscience. Beulah lay most of the night

196

thinking about how to get rid of Shep. There were pictures of Louis with a gun floating across Shep's brown eyes when Beulah stared into them in the early morning. Someone had to die after what had happened.

It was four o' clock that afternoon when she heard the shot. She put her knuckles in her mouth. Louis had never refused her anything.

'She's too old, her leg will never heal,' Beulah said, and many other lame things, besides. Louis looked at her sadly. Beulah could do what she liked with him.

She wondered what he was doing at that moment, the gunshot still resounding in his ears. Were Shep's eyes staring up at him? Where would he bury her? He had not wanted to kill Shep. Yet he had not argued. 'You have to be brave, Louis,' Beulah had told him and she went out to the shed. She put the gun into his hand. They had not spoken since.

Supper went on forever, neither Louis or Beulah were able to eat. Louis had put out all Beulah's favourites; Spam, white shop-bread, chicken and ham spread, Kerry creams and lemonade. Louis tried to put his hand on Beulah's but she pulled away from him.

'Are you sorry I shot Shep?' he asked, puzzled.

'No, I am not sorry,' Beulah said, hoarsely and pushing back her plate went up to bed early. She sat in the half-light, not bothering to light the Aladdin lamp. She did not think about Shep. She wished that she had a mirror, that she had perfume. She worried about the smell of Sunlight soap from her body. Louis had used up the last of the Swan soap. And there were even prettier soaps tied up with ribbon in Mrs Tobin's chemist shop. She brushed her hair over the sheets. It fell over the white covers in black ripples. She sat still in the middle of her hair as someone approached her bedroom door. She recognised the

197

same eager stumble from the night before. She held her breath. The door creaked open to reveal Louis's face.

Beulah edged to the far side of the bed. She pulled up her feet under her nightgown as Louis approached the bed with his hand outstretched. 'There's no need to be ashamed, Beulah,' he sat down on the bed and took hold of a ribbon of black hair and pressed his lips against it. A toad or a snake on the bed could not have been worse. Beulah shuddered.

'I thought that it would be all right now,' Louis put his small hand on her ankle.

Beulah pushed his hand away. Louis looked surprised but he was not angry with her. He could see that she was very nervous. He knew that she was shy, he was shy too.

'I was nervous myself last night,' Louis began. He would have liked to take her hand. He wanted to reassure her but the wild look in her eyes prevented him.

'Last night?' Beulah looked at him, surprised.

Louis's eyes were cloudy with love and desire. It was understandable for Beulah to be very shy about what had happened. But the sheer surprise and now the revulsion in her eyes troubled him. Minutes went by. They looked at each other. Louis's eyes cleared slowly and painfully until they were icy blue with comprehension. Beulah was about to speak again but he put his hand up to stop her.

Nothing she could say would change things now. She had gone out to meet someone else. His sudden white face and deadly clear eyes were terrible to Beulah. She tried to say that she had done nothing wrong but Louis pushed her away, 'It's not just me, it's Shep,' he said.

He left the house, Beulah heard the front door click. She wanted to follow him but she couldn't. She sat on the edge of the bed, staring at her long bare feet. She had not meant to hurt Louis.

Beulah lit the Aladdin lamp, she paced, she shivered. She wondered what it was like to smoke a cigarette. Shep's brown eyes merged into Louis's blue eyes. In the dark pupils, Beulah saw Louis walking down the field with the shotgun and the back of Shep's soft hairy neck. She saw it all as if she had been there. As time went on, she grew afraid, not for Louis, afraid for herself in the dark house all alone. Then she heard a dog barking. At first, she wasn't sure, then she heard it again. Out the front, a prolonged baying that she couldn't fail to recognise.

Alive after all and Louis was bringing her back. He'd known all the time that Beulah would be sorry afterwards. Louis thought of everything. Beulah ran to get her long grey coat and shoved her bare feet into her black shoes. She didn't stop to tie the laces as she ran, the laces clittered around her legs and on the linoleum.

It was all right. She could forget about Joe Costello now. She struggled with the bolts on the front door. Her shoes crunched on the gravel outside the front of the house. It was cold and the night was completely clear, unlike the one before. A half moon was in the sky, a perfectly symmetrical half. As if someone had sliced it with a sharp knife. 'Shep, Shep, tsk, tsk, tsk,' called Beulah into the cold pure silence and then she went round the back.

The wrought-iron of the front gates was cold against her fingers but the gates opened easily. Beulah smiled, thinking about Louis and his 3-IN-ONE oil. 'There's a good swing off them now, have a go yourself, Beulah.'

Around the back there was still no sound, nothing but the creak of branches and the faint moan of cattle from the field beyond. Beulah crept past the farm sheds warily, every minute expecting Shep and Louis to jump out and surprise her. She continued down the back as far as the stream and then followed the stream around to the millwheel. That was where they would be waiting. Shep and Louis. The air was heavy with lilac. Rats and small creatures were scurrying around in the bushes. Beulah wasn't afraid yet. She barely registered the sounds until she heard the creaking of the rope.

When Beulah looked up, she saw Louis hanging, his slight figure floating in his black clothes. She stood for a few moments under the creaking rope, looking at his still white face, his dead eyes. Slowly, her hands went up to cover her mouth, her eyes, her ears. Then she ran. She found herself at the top of Stanley's field; at her feet, in an orange crate, Shep's body awaited burial.

Chapter Twenty

Danny Fox found Beulah, wandering in the early morning and brought her back to his house. She never knew what he was doing out so early or what he was at in Stanley's field. She couldn't remember much of the night, she'd been running in circles for part of it, humming a strange tune to herself. If she ran and hummed long enough then Louis's body might disappear. But however long she ran and hummed, she never went back to check if Louis's body was gone. She knew it could no more disappear than Shep's snarling corpse could come to life in the orange crate. So she ran and she ran until she lay down. A sort of darkness fell over her. When she woke from this, she ran again. To the stream this time. It was shallow and she tried to lie face down and smother herself that way. But her body kept forcing her up for air. Then Danny Fox came and caught her by the shoulders.

It made her ashamed even now to remember that she had leant against him as he led her along the field. She said it wasn't her fault. She had been given a life that was impossible and all she wanted was a bit of happiness and was that too much to ask? Of course it was too much to ask and she had punished them all, Louis, Shep and herself. Hell was on earth, on Hollywood farm, there was no doubt about that. Danny talked away to her, 'How in the name of God could it be your fault? You have had a shock and I'm going to get the doctor.'

Beulah had never been inside Fox's small dim cottage. She hardly knew Maggie Fox, who stood, stooped in her black shawl at the half door as if she was expecting them, 'Take the trap and go straight for Joe Costello,' she said to Danny and then she caught Beulah's arm and gently led her to sit on a wooden settle by the fire. She made the tea without talking, and Beulah drank it scalding hot, grateful for Maggie's silence. Whether Maggie was being tactful or disapproving, she wasn't sure.

It was a month later when Maggie made Danny promise on her future grave never to reveal to a soul what had happened the night of Louis's death or about Joe Costello's attendance on Beulah at the cottage, for the three days following Louis's death. By then, Maggie Fox was full of gratitude, Beulah was dressing her ulcerated leg twice a week. Danny wouldn't promise, saying that he didn't need to because he would never tell on Beulah the longest day he lived. He said that he was insulted even to be asked and he slammed out the back door in a sudden rage.

That morning after her first scalding cup of tea, Beulah asked for a bowl of water to wash. 'Open that door, there,' Maggie nodded her head at a cupboard door set into the wall when she came back with the bowl. When Beulah opened the door there was the staircase painted brown, leading to the upstairs bedroom. Maggie followed Beulah into the small room with its narrow white bed. She put down the bowl on the only other bit of furniture, an upside-down tea chest. 'What need have you to be washing now? In the treacherous month of May?' Maggie Fox asked rhetorically before leaving the bedroom.

Maggie Fox continued to mutter to herself as she went slowly down the stairs, 'Touched in the head every one of them. Small wonder that they're dropping like flies!'

Ten minutes later, Maggie Fox puffed up the stairs again. 'The doctor is coming now, girl, and he'll know how to treat you for the shock.'

Joe Costello's face was white as he came up the narrow stairs. 'We have taken the body back to the farm, I will have to write a death certificate,' he said, shortly. 'But the Foxes have agreed, in fact, they are insisting that you stay here for a while.' Beulah thought that he was angry with her until she noticed his hands were shaking so much he could hardly get his doctor's bag open. 'I'm going to give you an injection.' Beulah helped him to roll up the sleeve of her nightgown and held her arm out obediently. She held her breath as the needle pierced her fine skin. She didn't know what injections did, but having an injection seemed drastic. Some injections even put you to sleep forever, she hoped that it was one of those.

Beulah slid into a delicious morphine trance. It started with a floating feeling in the pit of her stomach. She felt no pain except a desire to talk to Joe Costello. She was glad that he was escorting her on her journey to the other side.

Joe Costello might have been innocently trying to humour his shocked patient when he took hold of her wrist to name the carpel bones, the scaphoid which was known as the 'snuffbox'. He showed her how to flex her thumb so that the little groove to hold snuff was created at the base. But he could hardly have been innocent when he traced the outlines of her scapulas and counted out every bone in her vertebral column. When Beulah realised that she was still on earth, she kissed his forehead, his temples and the bumpy bit on the side of his jaw. His *frontal bone, parietal bones and the angle of the mandible*. Joe pointed out the clicky bits in front of the opening of his ears. These were the *temporo-mandibular joints*, they were very sensitive. When Beulah brushed her fingers against them, lightly, Joe got an impression of electricity passing up the side of his face.

Beulah didn't know what Danny or his mother had seen or what they knew, she remembered very little of the Foxes' apart from Joe and that narrow white bed. The Foxes' nasal droning

203

of the rosary each evening in the candlelight, forming a background to Joe Costello's naming of the bones. *Scaphoid, lunate, pisiform, triquetral, hamate, capitate, trapezium, trapezoid.* He said that time was relative, he held her pale wrist in his even whiter fingers. Their shyness was a light between them. They had all the time in the world, he told her.

When Beulah left Fox's cottage she set to cleaning her own house with more vigour than she ever had before. She went into the hardware shop and bought the cockroach-killer herself. The men behind the counter didn't laugh at her, they didn't even look at her. They served her with their eyes lowered, like shy princesses from *The Arabian Nights*.

Hester came, and then Hester stayed when they realised Beulah was expecting, 'It will be part of Louis. Aren't you lucky now, after all?'

'*The Lord gave and the Lord hath taken away; blessed be the name of the Lord,*' said the Reverend Moylan. 'He's given you back double, Beulah. He is watching over you and our community.'

New Poleites were needed always, they were not a fertile tribe. Prayers and prayers and prayers were said over the twins. Everybody was overjoyed and Beulah was still stunned when she entered motherhood. Leah was dark like herself. John grew up an absolute replica of Louis. Han and Bertie took great pleasure and comfort in the new babies until they reached the age of two, then Han and Bertie's hearts gave up within a month of each other. 'They were always united, the perfect loving husband and wife,' said Reverend Moylan, praising them at the funeral.

Chapter Twenty-One

Every day, Beccy washed herself with cold water and sprayed Diorissimo perfume behind her ears. She read the Bible and dressed in black and grey. Then one morning, Beulah wheeled into the parlour. 'Look what I've got!' she announced, indicating a folded woollen garment which was lying across her knees.

'Ah no! It's not!' exclaimed Hester her eyes filling with tears.

'It is, so,' said Beulah proudly.

'What is it?' asked Beccy.

'Beulah's wedding dress, I made it fifty years ago,' said Hester proudly, turning it inside out and examining the seams. 'It is nearly as good as new, you know.' She looked up at Beulah, 'I thought that you had thrown it out.'

'I had, too, but didn't I catch Danny Fox trying to steal it out of the dustbin. I decided then I was going to keep it after all. I washed it in cold water and Lux flakes, isn't it grand!' Beulah fingered the pale grey lace at the collar. 'Come on, now, upstairs and get into it,' she handed the dress to Beccy.

'Do you mean it?' asked Beccy, eagerly taking the soft bundle.

'I have a mind to see what I looked like before,' said Beulah.

Beccy floated down the stairs, looking taller and thinner in the long length of grey. Hester brushed out Beccy's plaits and dividing the hair in a new dead-straight centre crease, wound the dark pile into a tight coil at the base of her neck, 'Like someone cut the head off *you*,' said Hester, as Beulah stared. Then the phone rang. As Beccy went to get it, Beulah thought that she saw the mass of hair slide as if it was going to fall.

Out in the hall, Beccy cried out, and for a few awful moments Beulah fixed her eyes on Hester's shaking jaw, sure that something had happened to Leah. When Beccy came back, she looked at their faces and quickly spoke. 'It is not that bad, but it is bad for Danny Fox. That was Nellie Sheehan, she said that he was seen going home blind drunk half an hour ago. Going from side to side of the road. Queenie is dead. She asked me to go down there, to see if he is all right.'

'Poor old Queenie,' said Hester.

'She was sixteen years of age,' said Beulah, her voice gone soft. 'He wouldn't take her to the vet for her final injection and he'll be sorry now, the poor fool. Take a couple of tins of steak-and-kidney pie from the press. He'll need them. And you can let on that I drank his old goat's milk if you like.'

'Will she be all right?' Hester wondered, as Beccy went into the hall and they followed her, Beulah wheeling her chair.

'No fear at all,' Beulah said, although she was suddenly worried herself. It seemed again like Beccy's hair was beginning to slide as she fumbled with the lock of the front door. 'She should have taken off that dress.'

'He'll hardly notice, will he?'

'He might. If she is not back in a half an hour, ring Nellie Sheehan. He might say things to her if he's drunk and in shock.'

'What kind of things.'

'Any kind of things at all, I suppose.' Beulah winced with pain and then relaxed again. What happened had happened. It was all her fault and it was none of her fault.

Beccy shut the back door. There was a soft delicious wind, it tickled the back of her neck and the side of her cheek. Dusk was

206

gathering and she decided to go by the road instead of the lane by the mill. She loved everything about the farm, all the different entrances and exits. She couldn't get enough of it, every day she patrolled the grounds, walked by the stream, touched the mill, put her hand on the stone wall between the two farms. She had hungered to come back for years while Leah stayed away.

Beccy wished that she owned it herself, she would love to be able to clean it and arrange things her own way, to make new curtains, plant sweet peas and strawberries. Why did Beulah resent her wanting the place? Beccy would care for Beulah and Hester, she didn't see why she couldn't inherit Hollywood farm. Leah didn't want it.

Beccy admired the tall wrought-iron gates as she passed through them. The leaves and branches bent and waved above her head as she walked up the lime-tree-lined avenue. At the top of the avenue she turned left, walked a bit, turned into Fox's boreen. The boreen was narrower and the grass in the centre of the track was like a dark velvet ruff. The country noises, dogs and cows and the scuttling in the bushes began to unnerve Beccy and she quickened her steps, breaking into a run as she came up to the cottage.

Danny was sitting in the gloom, blaming himself for Queenie's death, he should have taken her to the vet, he should have fed her fresh meat. 'Who knows in the name of God what they put into them ould cans!' Beccy was moving around the dim kitchen trying to find the light switch. 'She was going to die anyway.'

'I could have been kinder,' Danny went on. 'I gave her Wagon Wheels even though I knew they were bad for her teeth just to be keeping in with her . . . oh!' he exclaimed as Beccy found the light switch behind a bundle of newspapers on top of two tea chests.

Danny sat with his mouth open, releasing further fumes of Murphy's stout. Beccy put her hand over her nose and mouth.

'You're after giving me an awful fright, the grey frock and all. Beulah used to come down here every day. She used to dress Mamie's leg. I told you that of course. But she was always spotless, she had very high standards. Down here in that dress and not a hair out of place, there is no doubt, she cheered us up a whole lot. We looked forward to seeing her and she seemed to look forward to seeing us, too. Joe Costello came one time and examined her during the rosary.'

'Examined her?'

'Sure, Louis's death was a desperate shock to her. She needed treatment. She was never the same after and I think she gave up the religion then. Not when John died, that's what everyone else thinks of course. She gave up the religion then, oh yes, Joe Costello was down here, instructing her. I gave him the "go ahead", I was always friendly with him since we were boys. Do you know, I thought that she might get married again.' Danny's eyes were fixed on the windowsill where a male blackbird was hopping in the twilight, expectantly.

Danny sounded regretful, 'And do you know afterwards, she wouldn't speak to me. It finished me for a long time, it did so.'

'Beulah is very fond of you, it is just her way, look, she sent these down.' Beccy showed him the two tins of steak-and-kidney pie. She thought it better not to mention that Beulah knew all about Queenie.

Danny seemed comforted. He spoke again. Waves of Murphy's vapours filled the air as he exhaled. 'Denny's Meats, by God. They are the best. I suppose Beulah was shy after. She was upstairs, Mamie was in the room behind the fireplace and I slept here on the settle. And the settle is where we used to kneel for the rosary when Joe Costello went upstairs to do the Naming of the Bones.'

'The Naming of the Bones?' echoed Beccy.

'The Naming of the Bones, that is right. He had to teach her all the words, it was a kind of a cure. He told me in confidence that it was a branch of hypnosis. Oh, he was a very educated man and hard-working too. He was right in the middle of getting ready to get married but he always found time for us.'

Danny spoke as if he and Beulah were part of the one family.

'And what did Joe think?'

''Tis hard to know, he was always serious and kind of breathless with rushing. Once I remember he said something to me and I never forgot it.'

'What was that?'

'I was codding him about getting married, I used to do that a lot, *When are you going for the high jump*? says I.' Danny's eyes were faraway now, they were looking far beyond the blackbird, far into the deepening blue of the evening.

'What did he answer?'

'He didn't answer me at all, he asked me a question.'

'What did he ask?'

'He asked me did I know the meaning of Beulah's name. I didn't. I asked him if *he* knew. He picked up his doctor's bag and he had his hand on the handle of the door to leave, when he answered.'

'What he did say?' Beccy asked. She fingered the three pearl grey buttons at the neck of her dress.

' "Paradise",' Danny answered. ' "Paradise", that was what he said. That was the meaning of her name, can you credit it? Paradise, that was what Joe Costello said, then off out the door with him to get married the following morning.' Danny stared into the dark blue of the evening, he didn't speak after that. He kept staring at the window while Beccy made the tea and heated the steak-and-kidney pie. He kept staring until the sky was black. Then he fell asleep and Beccy walked home in Beulah's old grey dress.

209

A NOTE ON THE AUTHOR

Martina Evans was born in 1961 and grew up in Co. Cork. She trained as a radiographer at St Vincent's Hospital, Dublin, and moved to London in 1988. She is the author of two novels, *Midnight Feast* (1996) and *The Glass Mountain* (1997), and of two collections of poetry, *The Iniscarra Bar and Cycle Rest* (1995) and *All Alcoholics Are Charmers* (1998). She was awarded an Arts Council of England Writer's Award in 1999.

A NOTE ON THE TYPE

The text of this book is set in Berling roman. A modern face designed by K. E. Forsberg between 1951–58. In spite of its youth it does carry the characteristics of an old face. The serifs are inclined and blunt, and the g has a straight ear.